"What are you going to do, Logan?"

Nicole asked. "Keep me chained here and run off every male visitor who happens to drive up the lane?"

Logan wished his inheritance were the only reason he felt so possessive of Nicole. But since that night he'd learned she was a virgin, he'd been torn between wanting to protect her and coveting her. It was crazy and yet he couldn't seem to control himself.

"If I have to. You're too young to think about a serious relationship."

"But I'm not too young to be your wife." She felt the need to remind him.

"I told you. That would only be a union on paper. Nothing else," he said curtly.

Nothing else, Nicole repeated to herself as her gaze traveled up and down his hard, lean body.

Then why did it feel like it would be so much more?

Dear Reader,

Happy New Year to you, and Happy Birthday to us! This year marks the twentieth anniversary of Silhouette Books, and Silhouette Romance is where it all began. Ever since May 1980, Silhouette Romance—and Silhouette Books—has published the best in contemporary category romance fiction, written by the genre's finest authors. And the year's stellar lineups across all Silhouette series continue that tradition.

In Romance this month, bestselling author Stella Bagwell delivers an emotional VIRGIN BRIDES story in which childhood nemeses strike *The Bridal Bargain*. ROYALLY WED, Silhouette's exciting cross-line series, arrives with *The Princess's White Knight* by popular author Carla Cassidy. A rebellious princess, her bodyguard, a marriage of convenience—need I say more? Next month, check out Silhouette Desire's Anne Marie Winston's *The Pregnant Princess* to follow the continuing adventures of the Wyndham family.

Plain Jane Marries the Boss in Elizabeth Harbison's enchanting CINDERELLA BRIDES title. In Donna Clayton's *Adopted Dad,* a first-time father experiences the healing power of love. A small-town beautician becomes *Engaged to the Doctor* to protect her little girl in Robin Nicholas's latest charmer. And *Husband Wanted—Fast!* is a pregnant woman's need in Rebecca Daniels's sparkling Romance.

In coming months, look for special titles by longtime favorites Diana Palmer, Joan Hohl, Kasey Michaels, Dixie Browning, Phyllis Halldorson and Tracy Sinclair, as well as many newer, but just as loved authors. It's an exciting year for Silhouette Books, and we invite you to join the celebration!

Happy reading!

Mary-Theresa Hussey

Mary-Theresa Hussey
Senior Editor

Please address questions and book requests to:
Silhouette Reader Service
U.S.: 3010 Walden Ave., P.O. Box 1325, Buffalo, NY 14269
Canadian: P.O. Box 609, Fort Erie, Ont. L2A 5X3

VIRGIN BRIDES

Stella Bagwell

THE BRIDAL BARGAIN

Silhouette
R O M A N C E™
Published by Silhouette Books
America's Publisher of Contemporary Romance

To Bettye, a special friend

SILHOUETTE BOOKS

ISBN 0-373-19414-5

THE BRIDAL BARGAIN

Copyright © 1999 by Stella Bagwell

All rights reserved. Except for use in any review, the reproduction
or utilization of this work in whole or in part in any form by any
electronic, mechanical or other means, now known or hereafter
invented, including xerography, photocopying and recording, or in
any information storage or retrieval system, is forbidden without
the written permission of the editorial office, Silhouette Books,
300 East 42nd Street, New York, NY 10017 U.S.A.

All characters in this book have no existence outside the imagination of
the author and have no relation whatsoever to anyone bearing the same
name or names. They are not even distantly inspired by any individual
known or unknown to the author, and all incidents are pure invention.

This edition published by arrangement with Harlequin Books S.A.

® and TM are trademarks of Harlequin Books S.A., used under license.
Trademarks indicated with ® are registered in the United States Patent
and Trademark Office, the Canadian Trade Marks Office and in other
countries.

Visit us at www.romance.net

Printed in U.S.A.

Books by Stella Bagwell

Silhouette Romance

Golden Glory #469
Moonlight Bandit #485
A Mist on the Mountain #510
Madeline's Song #543
The Outsider #560
The New Kid in Town #587
Cactus Rose #621
Hillbilly Heart #634
Teach Me #657
The White Night #674
No Horsing Around #699
That Southern Touch #723
Gentle as a Lamb #748
A Practical Man #789
Precious Pretender #812
Done to Perfection #836
Rodeo Rider #878
*Their First Thanksgiving #903
*The Best Christmas Ever #909
*New Year's Baby #915
Hero in Disguise #954
Corporate Cowgirl #991
Daniel's Daddy #1020
A Cowboy for Christmas #1052
Daddy Lessons #1085
Wanted: Wife #1140
†The Sheriff's Son #1218
†The Rancher's Bride #1224
†The Tycoon's Tots #1228
†The Rancher's Blessed Event #1296
†The Ranger and the Widow Woman #1314
†The Cowboy and the Debutante #1334
†Millionaire on Her Doorstep #1368
The Bridal Bargain #1414

Silhouette Special Edition

Found: One Runaway Bride #1049
†Penny Parker's Pregnant! #1258

*Heartland Holidays Trilogy
†Twins on the Doorstep

STELLA BAGWELL

sold her first book to Silhouette in November 1985. Now, nearly forty novels later, she is still thrilled to see her books in print and can't imagine having any other job than that of writing about two people falling in love.

She lives in a small town in southeastern Oklahoma with her husband of twenty-eight years. She has one son.

Dear Reader,

Having just celebrated my twenty-eighth wedding anniversary, I can easily say it's been a long time since I was a new bride. But I can also testify that no matter how many years pass, romance and passion between a husband and wife who truly love each other never fades, it only deepens with time.

On the day of my recent anniversary, someone remarked that twenty-eight years was a record for a marriage in these days and times. I hope that isn't true. Because I happen to believe a marriage can endure through any times, good or bad, as long as a man and wife are willing to put their spouse's needs before their own. When a lifetime of love is the reward, there are no sacrifices.

As for the heroine of this book, Nicole's virginity is something she proudly gives to her husband as a gift, and in doing so, she learns just what a powerful and precious bond the love between a man and a wife truly is.

I hope you get as much enjoyment from reading *The Bridal Bargain* as I did writing it, and that each of you is blessed with love and happiness.

Best wishes,

Stella Bagwell

Chapter One

Nicole Carrington stared numbly out the window, past the large pillared porch and down the long alley lined with ancient, moss-draped live oaks. The last car of mourners had finally disappeared from sight, but the ordeal of losing her mother was far from over.

The presence of the man sitting behind her on a brocade-covered settee constantly reminded her of the sober fact. Four long years had passed since Logan McNally had stepped foot on Belle Rouge Plantation. She'd resented his presence then and she resented it even more now.

Across the parlor, Logan openly watched his young stepsister. She'd changed drastically since he'd last laid eyes on her, and the difference jarred him in a way he'd never expected.

She was not the tall, awkward teenager whom he'd left on the front porch, glaring after him with a pair of resentful brown eyes. Her slender body had blossomed into that of a sensually curved young woman, one who moved with a grace and confidence that seemed beyond her twenty-two years.

Beneath the black netting draped from the brim of her hat, her features were as delicate as hand-painted porcelain. Her tawny blond mane was no longer wild and neglected. It was now as shiny as satin and coiled loosely at the back of her neck in a style that was both demure and fitting for the somber day. The small hands gripping the white magnolia blossom were perfectly manicured and unadorned with jewelry.

If he'd not known she was a Carrington, he would've considered her the perfect image of a true Southern lady. But the outward poise couldn't totally camouflage the breeding beneath. Like mother, like daughter, he thought sourly. Some poor fool would eventually be taken in by her beauty. But not Logan. He knew exactly who and what she was.

Eventually, Nicole forced herself to turn away from the window. As she did, she was shocked to discover her legs had grown shaky. Throughout the funeral services and up until this point, she'd been strong and composed. She couldn't wilt now. Not with Logan watching her like a cat after a cornered bird.

She started carefully toward a chair that would put her a safe ten feet away from him. Halfway there a strong arm came around the back of her waist.

"Are you all right?"

The deep male voice jolted her and her gaze flew up to his hard, dark profile. Logan had been back at Belle Rouge for two days. During that time, he'd not bothered with one word of sympathy. It seemed hypocritical that he should play the part of the concerned relative now.

"I will be once I sit down. Please don't disturb yourself," she said curtly.

His gray eyes scanned her pale face and then he muttered a curse word. "More guests might arrive to offer their condolences. It would look pretty damn stupid if they found you lying here on the floor in a dead faint."

Her nostrils flared with contempt. Logan McNally was wildly attractive, with coffee-brown hair and equally dark skin. His pale gray eyes were fringed with thick black lashes and possessed the piercing quality of a knife blade. Above his strong, dented chin was a pair of perfectly chiseled lips. And as if his striking features weren't enough to set female hearts aflutter, he was blessed with a tall, lean, broad-shouldered body. But Nicole was immune to Logan's physical charms. She'd learned that underneath all that blatant masculinity was an arrogant rogue who cared for no one but himself.

"Still worried about impressions, I see," she said, her Louisiana drawl dripping with acid. "Well, I assure you I can get through the rest of this day without embarrassing you."

His hand tightened on her waist as he deliberately urged her down in the chair. "I wasn't worried about being embarrassed."

She made a mocking sound in her throat. "I'm sure. My mother and I have been an embarrassment for you since day one. So I guess this must be a time of celebration for you. At least you're rid of one of us. And who knows, in the next day or so you might get even luckier and I'll step in front of a car, or a lightning bolt will strike me."

His features tight, he straightened away from her. "You're sounding hysterical now," he growled.

Reaching up, she pulled two hat pins from the heavy coil of her hair. "I'm sure you'd like that, too," she said coolly. "You'd enjoy having me committed to a mental asylum. Then nothing would be standing in the way of you and Belle Rouge."

She swept the wide-brimmed hat from her head and as she did, Logan's eyes fixed on the elegant picture she made sitting there in the parlor in her expensive black suit and high heels. The last time he'd seen her she'd been a starry-eyed eighteen. Now she was twenty-two and already cynical. Logan couldn't help but wonder what had made her that way. But since his father had died four years ago, he'd not kept in contact with Nicole and her mother, even though the two women had continued to live here in his family home.

Sighing, he walked over to a small table holding a cut-glass decanter of Kentucky bourbon. He poured himself a small amount, took two long swigs, then turned back to her. "I can see that you've grown up on the outside, Nicole. But it's obvious your thinking hasn't matured along with your body."

Fury swamped her, but she kept it carefully hidden. Above anything else, she didn't want to let him think he could rile her as he once did. She was a grown-up woman now. Not a little teenager he could charm or insult whenever he took the notion. And he needed to know that.

"I suppose now you're going to try to tell me you have no interest in Belle Rouge."

He lifted the shot glass to his lips and tossed back the last of the bourbon. The fire it spread through his stomach did little to block out the odd emotions jabbing at him. He didn't want to feel any sympathy for this young woman. In one sense she'd virtually taken his father and his home away from him. And yet he didn't want to think of her aching with grief. Nor did he like seeing the cold, bitter woman she was showing him.

"I'd be lying if I told you I wasn't interested in Belle Rouge. This plantation has been in the McNally family since the 1700s. I don't intend to let it end with me."

With a tired grimace she rose from the chair and started out of the room. Logan immediately called after her, "Where are you going?"

"To lie down. You can play lord of the manor for a while. Since that's what you think you want to be," she added.

Before he could say more, Nicole quickly escaped to her bedroom upstairs and removed her clothing. Then, donning a thin cotton robe, she lay down on her four-poster and turned her face toward the wide double window looking out over the pecan grove.

It was the first of April and spring had well and truly arrived in the Cane River bottomlands. Flowers were blooming in glorious color in the gardens at the back of the house, and most of the cane fields were already planted.

Normally, Nicole loved this time of year, but she was both mentally and physically drained. Since her mother had suffered a stroke a little more than two years ago, Nicole's life had been a continuous juggling act as she tried to finish her college degree and care for the only true family member she had left in the world. Losing Simone to a second stroke had been a nightmare. And what was worse, the nightmare wasn't going to end until Logan went back to Shreveport or Nicole moved out.

Somehow she must have slept, because when she opened her eyes some time later, the room had grown dark and she was cold. Wearily, she pushed herself to her feet and walked over to the dressing table. Her hair had worked loose from its coil and now tumbled onto her shoulders in a swirl of tawny waves. She pushed it back from her face, then leaned closer to the mirror and let out a groan of disgust.

She looked ashen and wilted. Nicole knew if her mother were still alive to see her, she'd be disgusted. Simone had been a beautiful woman and had always taught her daughter to take pride in her physical appearance. Only last week her mother had sat at this very dressing table while Nicole had fashioned her hair in a smooth French twist.

Sinking onto the vanity bench, she covered her face with her hands and tried to block her silent tears. She had to face the fact that Simone was gone, and that she was well and truly alone now.

Nicole was unaware that anyone was near until she felt two strong hands curving around her shoulders.

"What are you doing in here?" Desperately she swiped at her wet eyes. The last thing she wanted was for Logan to think she was trying to garner his sympathy.

"I knocked on the door, but apparently you didn't hear me," he said, then added, "I've made sandwiches. I thought you might want to eat."

Her first inclination was to tell him she couldn't eat. Especially with him. But she didn't want to appear any weaker than she already had. And the fact that he'd come upstairs after her was the kindest gesture she could remember him making in a long time.

"I'll get dressed and be down in a minute or two," she told him.

Back in the kitchen, Logan set out plates and silverware on the small farm table, then poured two glasses of iced tea. It had been years since he'd felt free to make himself at home here at Belle Rouge. And he deeply regretted that it had taken the death of Nicole's mother to allow him free rein. Whatever Nicole thought, he'd not wanted the woman to die. For years he'd wanted her out of his home and his father's life, but he'd never wished ill of her or her daughter. Yet he doubted he'd ever convince Nicole of that. She truly believed he hated her. And maybe at one time he had hated her a little—when he'd been very young and needed a father, and she'd come along and usurped Lyle's affection and attention. But those feelings had left him long ago. Now he simply didn't know what he felt for Nicole, or what he was going to do with her.

Her light footstep sounded on the tile, and Logan turned away from the cabinet counter to see her entering the large room. She'd donned a pair of jeans and a pale blue T-shirt that buttoned down the front. His gaze lingered briefly on the rounded swells of her breasts, then lifted to her face. It was pale and drawn, her eyes red and puffy from her earlier tears. Yet the marks of grief could not dim her beauty.

He cleared his throat, then said, "I've already poured iced tea. But maybe you'd rather have soda or coffee."

"The tea is fine," she replied as she took a seat.

He carried a tray of sandwiches over to the table and

slipped into the chair opposite her. "There's bologna or ham. Take your pick."

She picked up a triangle of bologna sandwich. "The refrigerator is still crammed with casseroles and desserts friends have brought over during the past few days," she remarked.

"I know. But I'm sick of all that."

So was Nicole. She wanted to get back to plain food. Even more, she wanted to get back to a normal daily routine. Yet she wasn't even sure where her home was going to be now that the reason for her being here was gone.

The two of them ate in silence for several minutes. Nicole stared out the window toward the flower garden. Among the well-tended flowers were a gazebo covered with honeysuckle vine, a goldfish pond and several birdbaths, which the birds shared with the pesky squirrels that invaded the pecan trees growing at the back of the house. Before Simone's debilitating stroke, Nicole had spent many hours tending the garden with her mother.

"So, what are your plans now?"

Logan's question jerked Nicole out of her bittersweet memories, and she stared at him as though she resented the intrusion.

"My plans? Mother has barely been laid in the ground and you want to know my plans?"

He grimaced. "I realize you don't want to think about these things just now, Nicole. But you need to. For your sake—"

"Don't you mean for yours? You don't have to pretend with me, Logan. I know you're worried that you're going to have me as—as an unwanted responsibility. So let me put your mind to rest. I can take care of myself.''

"And how do you intend to do that? Do you have plans to get married?''

She scowled. "Married? Certainly not! I realize we live in the South, but surely even you don't think a woman has to have a husband to survive in this world.''

His gray eyes made a lazy inspection of her face. "No," he said slowly. "But you might have a man you're serious about.''

"Sorry. I've been too busy with college and caring for Mother to date anyone exclusively.'' At least, not since Bryce, she thought bitterly. Even now, after two years, Nicole still burned at the humiliation he'd put her through. She'd fallen hook, line and sinker for his words of love and adoration. She'd truly believed he wanted to marry her and live with her the rest of their lives. But in the end she'd learned he hadn't really been interested in a real future with her. All he'd wanted were a few romps in the hay, and when she wouldn't comply, he'd dumped her. "Besides," she added with a toss of her head, "I don't know that I'll ever want to get married.''

One of Logan's dark brows arched skeptically, but he said nothing.

She swallowed the last bite of her sandwich, then looked at him. "I suppose you'll be wanting me to move out soon.''

Logan leaned back in his chair and folded his arms across his chest. While she'd been resting he'd changed out of his dark suit and into a short-sleeved cotton shirt and a pair of blue jeans. Now Nicole's gaze dropped from his stoic face to his bare arms. They were corded with muscles and covered with fine black hair. A thin, expensive watch was strapped around his left wrist, but there were no rings on his hands. Which didn't surprise her. In spite of Logan's money, he was not a flashy man. And she couldn't help but admire him for that.

"Who said anything about you moving out?"

Both her brows lifted with surprise. "No one had to. It's obvious Belle Rouge is in your hands now," she said. Suddenly feeling far more anxious than she should be, she rose from the table and walked restlessly over to the door leading out to the back porch. It was open, and she could hear the night sounds of frogs and crickets singing in the garden.

"I understand you've been doing all the bookkeeping for the plantation since you graduated from college."

She glanced over her shoulder to see that he was still sitting at the table. She hoped he stayed there. It made her far too jumpy to have him anywhere near her. And above all she didn't want him to know just how much he affected her.

"That's right. Why? Are you planning on calling in an auditor to make sure I didn't skim off some of the profits?"

"No. I would like for you to keep on doing the job. Unless you don't want to."

Shocked, she whirled around to stare at him. "What do you mean? This plantation is—"

"Is partly yours now. Or didn't you know that?"

Stunned by his disclosure, she jerked her head back. "No. I—had no idea. Are you..." Moving back into the room, she walked to within a couple of feet from where he was sitting. "Are you being honest with me or is this some sort of cruel joke?"

This time it was Logan's turn to be surprised. From the look on Nicole's face it was obvious she'd truly known nothing about her inheritance. "Nicole, do you mean to tell me you didn't know what was in my father's will? It wasn't sealed. You could have looked at it any time after he passed away."

She shook her head again. "No. I didn't expect any of it to pertain to me. I knew that as long as Mother was alive we'd be allowed to live here. But other than that I thought this place was...all yours. You are the only child of Lyle McNally. And both his wives are dead now."

"You're forgetting you were his stepdaughter," Logan pointed out.

She moved over to a row of cabinets and leaned heavily against the counter. "Stepchildren rarely get honorable mention. Besides, I didn't expect anything from Lyle. He'd already given me a good home and education. It was far more than I would've ever had if Mother and I had still been living on our own. You and I both know that."

Oh, yes, he knew Simone Carrington had come from a poor family, just outside of Lafayette. His father had met her in Natchitoches, where she'd been working as a waitress in a diner.

Logan's lips twisted. "Apparently my father wanted you to have more. Or me less. I suppose you can look at it however you want to. Either way, a quarter of Belle Rouge is yours."

Nicole couldn't believe what she was hearing. She wasn't sure she wanted to hear it. She loved Belle Rouge. The plantation had been her home since she'd been twelve years old. But now that both her mother and stepfather were gone, she felt as if she was an interloper. Certainly Logan thought of her that way.

With a faint moan, she turned and headed out the door and across the screened-in veranda. Several yards behind the house, she sank onto a wrought-iron bench, situated beneath the massive arms of a live oak.

Belle Rouge was partly hers! What was she going to do?

Nicole was so deep in thought she didn't know Logan was anywhere around until he sat down on the bench beside her. Instantly she stiffened and turned her head away from him.

"Are you crying?" he asked roughly.

"No." Her mind was spinning with too many questions for her to be shedding tears.

Relieved at her curt answer, he continued, "Then what's the matter? Do you want to leave Belle Rouge? Is that what you've been planning?"

"No," she blurted instinctively, then bit down on her lip. She shouldn't have been so truthful with him. "I mean...well, the only thing I've had on my mind was Mother."

He sighed and for the thousandth time cursed his father for putting him in such a position. He didn't want to have to deal with Nicole Carrington. Not financially nor emotionally. Yet if he didn't abide by the terms of the will, he stood the chance of losing all of Belle Rouge.

"I'm sure that's what you'd like me to do," she added before he made any sort of reply. "So don't worry. I'll start packing tomorrow if that's soon enough."

The quiet weariness in her voice cut into him, though he didn't know why. He'd never pretended to like her or her mother. When he'd first learned of Lyle's plan to marry Simone, he'd been dead certain the woman was out to get a part of the McNally money, or even worse, a part of the plantation. Desperate to keep his father from making such a foolish mistake, Logan had brazenly gone to Simone and offered her a generous check to leave town and never come back.

Simone had refused, of course. Logan could still remember how the woman had thrown the check back at him. Yet frozen even deeper in his memory was the sight of Nicole, who'd crept into the room unnoticed by the two adults. Until this day, no one had ever looked at him with such pure venom as Nicole had.

At the time, Logan had convinced himself he didn't really care what the Carrington females had thought about him. Immediately after Lyle had married Simone, he'd left and never come back. At least, not to live. For his father's sake, he'd come back on brief occasions, but those visits had always been strained. For the most part, he'd tried to sever all his ties to Belle Rouge. Still, he'd not been able to forget the place or the people living there. Including Nicole.

"No. I don't want you to start packing," he told her. "You're going to live right here. And so am I."

Nicole's head whipped around and she stared at him in the semidarkness. "You must be kidding! Please tell me you are!"

He shook his head with a finality that left Nicole cold. "I'm not the kidding sort."

"No. I guess not," she said mockingly.

He studied her hard expression, then heaved a heavy breath. "Look, Nicole, I know you have it in your head that I detest you. But that's not the case. I don't...really even know you."

"Don't try to gloss things over, Logan. I wasn't quite a teenager when you came to our house and tried to buy my mother off, but I still remember it vividly. You deliberately hurt and insulted her by offering her a check to leave town, leave your father behind. And I'll not forget that, Logan. Not now. Not ever!"

"I was only trying to protect my father and our home," he countered.

She snorted with contempt. "By trying to get rid of the woman he loved?"

His hard features went even more rigid. "Did you ever stop to consider what I must have been feeling, having my father wed his mistress and have her—"

"Go ahead, say it," she dared him. Rising to her feet, she planted her hands on her hips. "Call me an illegitimate child. If you think that's going to hurt me, you're sadly mistaken. She couldn't help it if my father promised to marry her, then deserted her."

Logan hadn't planned on hashing out the bitter past with Nicole tonight or anytime, for that matter. They couldn't undo it. Yet he couldn't bear to have her making him the villain. "You're probably right about that," he conceded. "But she could have stayed away from my father. He was a married man, but she didn't care. She broke up my parents' marriage and drove my mother to alcoholism."

Nicole said tightly, "Your mother was drinking long before we ever came into the picture. And your father was sick of it. That's why he turned to Mother in the first place."

"You couldn't know that! You were only a child at the time!"

Nicole tossed her head. "I was practically a teenager. And after I grew up I heard Lyle talk about it many times. Clara was from Chicago. This Southern life was too slow for her. She hated it and wanted to leave. And because Lyle wouldn't, she began to hate him, too."

"So he'd have you believe," he retorted.

The sarcasm in his voice filled Nicole with fury. "You're not human. And I'll not live another day on this plantation with you!"

She turned and started back toward the house. She hadn't taken two steps before Logan's hand clamped down on her arm and jerked her back to him.

"These past two days I was beginning to get the impression you'd grown up since I've been away," he muttered through clenched jaws. "But I can see now that you haven't. You're still just a silly little virgin—"

She ripped her arm free of his grasp. "There's nothing silly about being a virgin. In fact, the more I'm around you, the more convinced I am that I *never* want a man to make love to me!"

Logan stared at her in surprise. He'd not actually used the word in a sexual sense. He'd been referring to her mental maturity. As for her body, he'd figured she'd given it away a long time ago. "Nicole, you're twenty-two, don't expect me to believe..." He shook his head with disbelief. "Surely you had a lover in college."

She sneered at him. "You think I'd *want* a lover, knowing all the pain and degradation my mother went through in her young life? No, thank you," she spat. "But as for your other opinion of me, I'll have to agree you're right, Logan. I'm silly for standing here wasting my time arguing with a bullheaded, arrogant—"

"Haven't you heard a thing I've been saying?" he interrupted. "You have to stay here on Belle Rouge. Otherwise—"

"I'll lose my part? Well, my dear stepbrother, I have a news flash for you. As much as I love Belle Rouge, I'm going to have to forfeit my inheritance. Living with you just wouldn't be worth it."

As soon as the last word was out, she turned on her heel and started toward the house. Once again, Logan caught her before she could take one long stride.

Nicole looked pointedly down at his hand gripping her shoulder. "I don't want you touching me. So stop it!"

One of his dark brows cocked upward and the corner of his mouth lifted in a sneer. "Why? You don't like for a man to touch you?"

Her features grew hard as she studied his mocking face. "No. Especially you."

Suddenly Logan forgot all about Belle Rouge and the reason they were arguing. The sight of Nicole's flashing brown eyes and moist, parted lips dared the primal male in him, and before he could stop himself, he clamped his free hand on her other shoulder and jerked her forward.

She fell with an awkward thump against his chest, and his hand came up to grab a handful of hair at the back of her head. With a tug on the red-gold strands, he forced her face to lift to his. At the same time Nicole's hands came up to shove against his chest. But she quickly discovered it was like pushing against a massive boulder.

"Let me go, Logan!"

"Why? Because you hate me?"

The dry curl of his lip infuriated her and she struggled even harder against him. "Yes!"

This time he chuckled, and Nicole stilled at the unexpected sound. Her brown eyes scanned his lean, angular features, and as they did she slowly began to smell him, feel him. The strong liking that followed terrified her. "You think that's funny? You think I'm a joke or—or something to play with?"

Rather than answer either question, he lifted his hand to gently push the tangle of hair off her forehead. For long moments his gaze held hers, then wandered over her hair, her cheeks and chin, finally coming to rest on her lips.

"A moment ago," he said quietly, "I couldn't believe you might actually be a virgin. But now I can see that you know nothing about being with a man—like this."

Much to her chagrin, she had to swallow before she could speak. "I'm not afraid of you," she whispered.

He grinned and the sight of his white teeth sent a mental shiver right down to Nicole's toes.

"No. I don't believe you are," he murmured. Then, still gripping her hair, he bent his head and found her lips.

Nicole was too shocked to do much but simply stand there and let his hard lips explore hers.

All in all it was not a lengthy kiss, but it was enough to leave her quaking. And the imprint of his lips burned her mouth long after he lifted his face.

"Satisfied? Can you let me go now?" she asked.

He was far from satisfied, and the last thing he wanted to do was let her go. But there was something in her shaky voice, something vulnerable and needy, that caught him off guard and stopped him from bending his head and kissing her again.

His eyes flicked over her one last time, then he relaxed his grip on her hair and stepped back. "We'll finish this in the morning," he told her.

She stared at him while wondering how it could feel so good to be touched by someone so bad.

"This *is* finished. As far as I'm concerned you can consider that a goodbye kiss. I'm leaving. You're welcome to Belle Rouge. I don't want any of it. And I especially don't want you!"

Logan had truly meant to walk away, but the last taunt she flung at him was too much to bear. Just as she started to turn her back to him, he lunged and caught her by the waist.

Nicole struggled wildly as he jerked her around and into his arms. But he was much too strong for her. In a matter of seconds his hand held her chin in a viselike grip.

"I think we should see how much you really mean that," he muttered.

The odd glitter in his eyes frightened her, but not nearly as much as the strange commotion going on inside of her. As his lips fastened roughly over hers, the only thing she could think was how much she really did want this man.

Logan had meant for the kiss to be a punishment, a lesson that when she goaded him she was playing with fire. But the instant he felt her lips soften and part beneath his, he forgot his intentions. His kiss suddenly turned to a needy search, and all too soon Nicole was rising on her tiptoes and sliding her arms around his neck.

It wasn't until his tongue had slipped between her teeth and she began to moan in her throat that he realized how far out of control both of them had become. And even then, he had to force himself to lift his head.

As he set her back from him, Nicole swayed on her feet. She gulped in several deep breaths, then, before he could stop her flight, turned and raced to the house as fast as her shaky legs would carry her.

Logan liked to think he wasn't a stupid or impulsive man, but as he watched her go, he realized he'd just been both with Nicole.

Now he had to think of a way to undo everything that had happened. Because he couldn't let her leave Belle Rouge. Not now. Maybe not ever.

Chapter Two

When Nicole opened her eyes the next morning, the gray light of dawn was just beginning to peek through the live oaks and dapple the cypress floor of her bedroom. Out on the landing she could hear Darcy, the housekeeper, singing an old country song about a man who'd done his woman wrong.

Nicole didn't figure Logan would take too kindly to being disturbed at such an early hour. But then she didn't really give a damn whether he got all the sleep he wanted. Logan was no longer her concern.

Wide awake now, she climbed out of bed, pulled a blue robe over her long cotton gown, then brushed her hair and tied it back with a white ribbon.

Outside her room, she spotted Darcy dropping an armload of dirty linen into a laundry basket. The older woman was tall and plump and had a wild mass of salt-and-pepper curls that usually fell unchecked into her faded blue eyes. But today she had scraped the whole lot into a bushy wad on top of her head.

The housekeeper had been working for Lyle Mc-Nally even before Nicole and her mother had come to live at Belle Rouge. The woman knew everything there was to know about the family, and what she didn't know, she wasn't bashful about finding out. Nicole had always loved her like a second mother.

"Good morning, Darcy."

The housekeeper smiled cheerfully. "Nicole! Did I wake you with my singin'? I'm sorry. I guess I just feel a little happier this morning. What with the funeral and all over maybe we can make this ol' place cheery again."

"I'm not so sure it will ever be cheery again, Darcy," Nicole said grimly. "But I hope so, for your sake."

The older woman frowned at her odd remark. "Well, for your sake, too," she said. "I know how much you loved your mama and how much you're gonna miss her. But she wouldn't want you sittin' around here cryin' and mopin'."

"I know," Nicole replied glumly. "But right now I don't know if I'll ever be happy again."

Darcy reached out and patted her on the shoulder. "Let's go down to the kitchen and I'll fix you some eggs and grits."

Nicole shook her head. "There's no need for you to bother. I'm not that hungry."

The other woman smiled with gentle patience. "There's no bother, honey. The grits are still warm from Mr. Logan's breakfast."

Nicole looked at her sharply. "You mean Logan has already been up and had breakfast?"

Darcy nodded. "He left the house a few minutes ago. Said he was going down to the cane fields. I don't know what for. They're too muddy to step foot in right now.''

Nicole frowned. ''He probably just wants to view his inheritance,'' she said dryly, then started down the steep stairs. ''I think I'll have some coffee and biscuits, after all. I've got a lot to do this morning.''

''Now what have you gotta do?'' Darcy asked as she picked up her laundry basket and followed behind Nicole. ''What you need is a nice, quiet rest for the next few days.''

''Can't do that. I've got to pack and find a place to live.''

''What are you talkin' about, honey? You live here at Belle Rouge and have ever since I can remember knowin' you.''

''That's right, Darcy. But things have changed since Mother's gone. This is rightfully Logan's place now. And I expect you know I could never live under the same roof with that man.''

The kitchen was filled with the warm, delicious scents of coffee and fried ham. Nicole poured herself a cup, then went to the cookstove, where Darcy had left buttermilk biscuits in an insulated basket.

She put two on a small plate and carried it and the coffee over to the same small table where she'd had sandwiches with Logan last night. As she slathered the biscuits with butter, then doused them with cane syrup, she tried to put that whole incident out of her mind. She'd behaved recklessly and totally out of character. Now all she could do was make sure it never happened again.

''Logan's been gone from here since he was a young man,'' Darcy said as she wiped the already spotless cabinet counter. "I can't see him happy here. Not after livin' in Shreveport all these years."

Nicole sighed. "I've thought the same thing. But Logan said last night he was going to live here. I guess the sudden control of the place has gone to his head."

Darcy tossed the cleaning rag into the sink, then jamming her hands on her ample hips, turned to look at Nicole. "That may be so. But Lyle would roll over in his grave if he knew you was thinkin' about movin' out."

Nicole shook her head as she chewed a bite of biscuit. "Well, I guess he'll just have to turn over in his grave. Because there's no possible way I can live with Logan."

Especially after the way she'd melted in his arms, she thought miserably. There was no telling what he was thinking about her. Probably that she was trying to get her gold-digging claws into him. The same way he thought her mother had done to his father.

Her expression full of concern, Darcy sank into the chair opposite Nicole. "Honey, I think you should study hard about all this. Havin' Logan around here might not be as bad as you think. Besides, I don't think he'll stay for long. He's got a lot of his mama in him. Belle Rouge was too quiet for her and will be for him, too. Especially without any women around to keep him entertained."

Nicole's fork paused in midair. "You make him sound like some sort of playboy. Is he that sort of man?"

Darcy shrugged. "I guess I shouldn't have said that, 'cause I don't really know. But that's what I hear. Anyway, the man is thirty-four years old and still hasn't married. That sounds like he's too busy playin' the field to me."

"Or he just doesn't like women," Nicole countered.

Darcy's laugh was mocking. "Yeah, and I don't like catfish and hush puppies for supper."

Nicole shoveled another bite of biscuit and syrup into her mouth while telling herself she didn't care one whit how many women the man had strung along behind him. She certainly didn't plan on being listed among his playthings. He'd caught her at a vulnerable moment last night and she'd momentarily lost her head. But she'd never repeat the mistake.

Popping the last of the biscuit into her mouth, she swallowed it down with a sip of strong, chicory-laced coffee. "Well, it's time I got upstairs and started packing."

Seeing Darcy's lips spread into a thin, disapproving line, Nicole reached across the table and patted the woman's thick hand. "Don't worry about it, Darcy. You're not going to lose your job. Logan knows he couldn't find anyone else to take care of this house like you do."

The older woman shook her head. "I don't care about any of that. I can always find some other job. This old place wouldn't be the same if you weren't here. I don't know that I'd want to stay if you left."

"Oh, Darcy, don't start in. This is bad enough as it is," she said with a groan. Then, so as not to let the other woman see her eyes welling up with tears, she rose from the table and hurried out of the room.

An hour later, Nicole had the contents of one entire closet tossed onto her bed, and was packing them carefully away in cardboard boxes.

In an effort to keep her spirits from sinking to rock bottom, Nicole deliberately hummed as she worked. It was better this way, she argued with herself. Nothing ever stayed the same. And nothing good could possibly come out of staying here and trying to hang on to a part of Belle Rouge. Logan would surely make things so miserable for her it wouldn't be worth the effort.

She was in the walk-in closet, digging out the last of the shoe boxes, when she heard a faint knock on the bedroom door.

"I'm in the closet, Darcy!" she yelled. "Did you find more boxes?"

The housekeeper didn't answer, and Nicole was about to decide she'd imagined the knock when a low, male voice sounded a few feet behind her.

Squatted on her heels, Nicole jerked her head around to see Logan standing in the doorway of the closet. He was dressed in old blue jeans and a faded red T-shirt. And before Nicole realized what she was doing, her gaze was sliding up and down his lean, masculine body.

"What are you doing?" he asked bluntly.

She rose to her feet so swiftly black dots momentarily swam in front of her eyes. "I'm..." She reached out and balanced herself by pressing her fingertips against the wall. "Packing," she finally managed to reply. "What does it look like?"

"Making a fool of yourself," he answered without preamble.

Her teeth ground together. "So you say," she said slowly, then moved toward him and the door. "If you don't mind, I'm very busy. Would you kindly let me out of here?"

He planted a hand on each side of the doorjamb.

"No. I think we can talk just as we are. With you in there and me out here," he drawled.

Nicole didn't like the idea of being cornered by this man. Even in a large room he made her feel suffocated. Like this, she could hardly breathe at all.

"As far as I'm concerned, we don't have anything to talk about, Logan. We said it all last night." She couldn't look him directly in the face. She was too overwhelmed with the embarrassing fact that she'd kissed him in a way she'd never kissed any man.

"No," he replied. "You did a lot of talking, when you should have been listening."

Her brows arched with wry speculation as she forced her eyes up to his face. "If I'd heard something worth listening to, I would have paid more notice."

With lazy insolence, Logan's gaze swept over her tangled blond hair and bare face. "You really are a smart-mouthed girl, aren't you?" he said softly.

She straightened her shoulders. "For your information, I'm not a girl and haven't been in some time."

The smirk of his lips said her need to remind him of her grown-up status was more than amusing. "If you're the woman you want me to believe you are, then you wouldn't be up here packing."

She gave a scoffing laugh. "I'm really surprised you're not downstairs breaking out a bottle of champagne. It must surely be a thrilling occasion for you to finally be finished with the Carringtons."

"I told you last night I wanted you to stay here. I still do," he said, yet even as he said the words, he wondered if he'd gone crazy. Logan never lost his head over a woman. Not after the lesson Tracie had taught him.

Logan had met the real estate agent not long after

his father had married and he'd severed himself from his family and Belle Rouge. He'd been lonely and vulnerable to her dark, glamorous looks and witty tongue. A few times in her arms had convinced him he was in love and that he wanted a family of his own. And even after he'd moved in with her, he hadn't known she'd had an unsuspecting husband overseas. Not until Logan naively asked her to be his wife.

To this day, the humiliation of that relationship sickened him. Just thinking of Tracie reinforced his vow to never let himself need or want any woman so much that it turned his world upside down. Yet last night, for those few moments under the live oak, Logan had forgotten everything. He'd wanted Nicole with a fierceness that still stunned him when he thought about it.

With a small sigh, Nicole shook her head. "I don't know what you're up to, Logan, but you'll never make me believe that line of...jargon. You want me here about as much as you want a hole in your head."

"I haven't stepped foot on this place in four years. How could you know so much about me?" he asked dryly.

She wished to heck he'd step aside and let her out of the closet. The more he talked, the more she felt the walls of the small room moving in. And she was terribly aware that if he took one step forward, they'd be cocooned together and she'd have no route of escape.

"Look, Logan, there's no use beating around the bush. You don't like me and I don't like you. I understand this was your father's plantation, and in spite of his generous will, it rightfully belongs to you." She made a hands-up gesture. "I have no argument with that. Nor will I have in the future. All I'm asking is that you step aside and let me get on with moving out."

He studied her face for so long that heat began to fill her cheeks. "You're saying you're willing to just let me have everything?" he asked. "After you've lived here nearly all your life? I can't believe that."

Her soft features were suddenly full of regret. "That's because you don't understand I'm nothing like you, Logan. Money isn't my main objective in life."

He was more curious than angry over her observation. "That's how you see me? As a man who simply wants money?"

"I see a lot of things in you, Logan. But yes, you've always had money and it will always be important to you."

Her admission shouldn't make him feel so disappointed. After all, he did like money, and for the past ten years he'd worked hard to accumulate more. Yet it irked him to think she believed he was that one-dimensional.

"So if you don't stay here, where do you think you'd go?" he asked. "Do you have money of your own?"

"I think my financial affairs are none of your business."

"I'm sorry. But they are."

She frowned with disbelief. "I beg your pardon?"

"The money you've been receiving from the profits of the estate were controlled by your mother, right?"

She nodded. "That's true. But mother is gone now. And I'm sorry, but I do have to have something to live on."

"Of course you have to have something to live on. But I think you should know that if you forfeit your shares of Belle Rouge, you'll lose that income. And even if you don't, the money is now under my control and will be until you marry or reach age twenty-five. Whichever comes first.''

She felt as if he'd sluiced her with a bucket of ice water. ''That can't be true! Just because Mother is dead doesn't mean you now have the right to control my finances!''

''I'm afraid you're wrong. Apparently my father wanted to make sure you had some sort of guardian until you reached a fit age to make financial decisions on your own. For now I'm that guardian.''

No, dear Lord, she prayed. If what Logan was saying was true, she couldn't move out of here. She couldn't do anything until she got a job and made a salary separate from the dividends she received from the plantation. And that could take months!

Suddenly she was quivering with rage. ''Why didn't you tell me this last night?'' she demanded.

''I tried to. You didn't want to hear anything I had to say.''

All she could remember about last night were his hateful, degrading words and the way he'd kissed her senseless. ''Well, what are you going to do about this? Surely you're going to allow me enough money to find a place of my own?''

His head swung back and forth, and Nicole felt panic rising up in her like a big, black thundercloud.

''You don't need a place of your own,'' he said. ''Your home is here.''

Nicole opened her mouth to blast him with all the fury raging inside her. But suddenly, through all her anger, she had the common sense to know she was wasting her energy trying to talk to Logan McNally. He considered his word etched in stone.

''Well, aren't you going to spit out whatever it is

you have to say?" he asked, when she continued to stare at him in silence.

"Please step aside and let me out of this closet."

The quiet calmness of her voice took him by complete surprise. He'd been mentally braced for shouts and threats, maybe even tears. And he was suddenly wondering if Nicole Carrington was a stronger woman than he'd first imagined.

Once he stepped out of the way, Nicole quickly brushed past him and went back to filling the boxes on her bed.

"What are you going to do?" he had to ask.

"Once I talk to my lawyer I'll let you know."

He snorted. "Be my guest. Talk to a lawyer all you want. But in the end I know he's going to advise you to stay here."

She jammed a stack of T-shirts into a box that was already partially filled with blue jeans. "Oh, really."

Logan continued to watch her hastily fold clothes and toss them into the first empty container she could find. She worked like a woman with a purpose, and he realized all his threats and warnings up to this point had done little to persuade her to give up the idea of leaving Belle Rouge. It was obvious she wanted to get away from him at any cost.

"Look, Nicole, I didn't come up here to fight with you about this. In spite of our bad beginning, I think we can make this thing work."

She dropped the blouse in her hand and turned to face him. As Logan looked into her brown eyes, he tried to ignore her dusky-pink lips. Yet the memory of their heady sweetness swamped his thoughts.

"And why would you want to make the effort of sharing this home with me?" she asked. Then, as a new thought occurred to her, she took a step toward him and folded her arms across her chest. "What is all this really about, Logan? We both know you don't want me here. So why all this talk about getting me to stay? There has to be some gain in it for you. I know it's not out of concern for my welfare."

Since Logan had worked as a professor at Louisiana State University, he'd faced some powerful men, many of whom could have made his job a living hell if they'd chosen to. He'd never wavered in their presence. But at this very moment, looking Nicole in the eye was almost more than he could stand.

"Do you think I'm some sort of monster, Nicole? I don't want you thrown out in the street!"

"We're out in the country. There aren't any streets around here. And no, you'd put up with me before you'd have people thinking you were that heartless!"

"But *you* think I'm heartless," he said, as he tried to ignore the urge to reach out and touch her.

Her lips thinned to a sneer. "I don't think it. I know it. So be honest with me, Logan. Why do you want me to stay here?"

How could he be honest with her? He'd stayed up half the night trying to decide how he really felt about Belle Rouge and Nicole. In the end he'd not been able to separate the two. Because like it or not, she'd become so much a part of this place, he couldn't picture one without the other. Nor could he have one without the other.

With a heavy sigh, he jammed his hands in the pockets of his jeans and walked over to the window. As he gazed down at the flower garden below, long-ago memories suddenly swamped him. The smell of the plowed fields, the sight of cane growing thick and green toward the sky, the rows of pecan trees heavy with nuts, the quiet, lazy meandering of the river. In Shreveport he'd not allowed himself to remember much about his home. But being back at Belle Rouge was making him realize how desperately he'd missed the place.

"If you'd been listening to me last night instead of hissing and clawing..."

Glancing over his shoulder, Logan was surprised to see Nicole's attention had drifted to a small music box cradled in her palms.

"Nicole? What is it?"

He walked over to her, and slowly she looked up at him. There was such a lost, mournful expression on her face that Logan wondered how he could possibly break any more news to her this morning. But he had to, he told himself. Bad timing or not, she needed to understand what Lyle's will meant to both of them.

"I—I'm sorry. I—my thoughts strayed for a few moments," she said huskily. Then, with a shake of her head, she carefully nestled the music box among her packed clothes.

"The music box has a special meaning to you?"

One corner of her lips curled upward in an expression that said she doubted he understood anything about sentimentality. And maybe she was right, Logan thought. The only thing he'd ever been sentimental over was Belle Rouge. And now those mawkish feelings were about to get him into a hell of a situation.

"My mother gave it to me for my birthday. Right after we came here to live. How long ago that seems now."

Logan was shocked at how much he wanted to take Nicole in his arms and comfort her. He had the reputation of being a hard man, and certainly he had no patience for emotional people. But something about Nicole being alone and full of grief hit a spot in his chest he hadn't even known was there.

"The loss will begin to ease. You just have to give it time, Nicole."

She looked at him as though she couldn't believe he was offering her any sort of sympathy. "You can't know how I'm feeling. Simone wasn't only my mother. She was my best friend, too."

"You're forgetting I've lost both my parents."

Nicole didn't want to get into that. Logan blamed Simone for his mother's death. Which was crazy. Clara had been driving drunk and had run head-on into a bridge abutment. Still, Logan reasoned his mother would've never been drinking if Simone and Lyle hadn't been having an affair.

"Yes. I realize that," she said with a sigh, then turned and headed back toward the walk-in closet.

As she brushed past Logan, he reached out and caught her by the arm. "Forget the damn packing. You're not going anywhere."

She looked down at his dark hand curled around the pale flesh of her upper arm, then lifted her gaze to his face. His nostrils were flared, his features rock hard. She wanted to hate him for his arrogance and lack of compassion for her feelings. And yet last night she'd glimpsed another side of him that she couldn't separate from the man facing her now.

"You haven't given me a good reason why I should stay."

He drew in a long breath, then slowly released it. All the while she could feel his gaze touching her face, her throat, her lips.

"I've given you several. The most important one

being that Belle Rouge has been your home for years and I know you don't want to leave it.''

Her brows arched ever so slightly. "You're right. I didn't want to leave it," she confessed. "Until I found out you were going to be staying.''

"I have no choice in the matter.''

His gray eyes were suddenly too much for her. She turned her head and stared at the half-packed boxes on her bed. "I don't have much choice, either. If you stay I have to go.''

"You must really hate me.''

Her head swung back around, and for a moment words failed her as she scanned his strong, angular features. Maybe she was crazy, Nicole thought, but for one brief second, she'd honestly believed she saw regret flicker in his eyes. Yet she knew she'd be a fool if she let herself soften toward this man.

"My mother taught me never to hate anyone. And that includes you, Logan. She wanted me to forgive you and forget about what you tried to do to us.''

His brows arched with speculation. "She called me once," he admitted, "not long after she and Dad married. She told me she'd like for us to put the past behind us and start over.''

"Why didn't you?" Nicole asked.

"I figured Dad had put her up to the phone call. I didn't believe she could really forgive me. You haven't.''

"You're right. I haven't. And I can't endure hashing all of this out with you every day of my life. And that's exactly what would happen if I stayed here.''

He hoped to hell she was wrong. He couldn't go through an emotional storm day after day with this woman.

Dropping her arm, he said, "All right, Nicole. I'm going to spell it out to you. My father has quartered the plantation between us."

Her brows shot up. As far as she knew, Lyle didn't have any other relatives. "Quartered? Who's getting the other half?"

"Our spouses."

Nicole's lips parted with shock. "Our spouses? Neither of us is married!"

"Obviously. But that's the way the old man had it written."

Nicole considered his words for long moments, then said, "Well, I still don't see that's much of a problem. I'll simply sign my two quarters over to you."

Logan's head swung back and forth. "It's not that simple."

"Why? It's my share. Can't I do what I want to with it?"

Logan let out a long breath. If only it was that easy, he thought. "First of all, both of us have to continue to live here for the next six months. Otherwise, the plantation will be donated to the state of Louisiana for historical purposes."

As Nicole slowly digested his words, everything suddenly became clear to her. And she didn't know if the pain in her chest was from anger or feelings of betrayal.

"So now we've finally gotten down to the truth of things," she said with quiet accusation. "If I don't live here, I'll not only lose my part of Belle Rouge, but you'll lose your part, too."

"I'm sorry. But that's the way the old man dealt the cards. And I realize you can't be any happier about it than I am."

"Happy!" she said with a bitter snort. "I'm sure I'll never know what it's like to be happy again. I can't imagine what Lyle must have been thinking! Why did my mother allow him to write such a ridiculous will in the first place?"

Many times through the years Lyle had urged him to come home, to live as a family with him and his new wife and stepdaughter. Logan had always refused. Not because he'd hated his father, but simply because he'd felt like an outsider. "I guess our parents had some odd notion that if we lived under the same roof it would force us to make peace with each other."

Nicole rolled her eyes and turned away from him. "It's crazy. Besides, when he made that will neither one of them expected to die so suddenly. And anyway, what if you and I were both married with families? We couldn't all live here in this house. Lyle should have thought about that."

Nicole walked back to the bed, and as she looked at the things she'd already packed, she threw up her arms in a gesture of disgust. "I honestly think your father must have gone off the beam." Suddenly another thought struck her and she glanced expectantly over her shoulder at him. "Do you think you could have the will changed?"

Logan grimaced. "You mean by trying to prove my father was mentally incompetent at the time he wrote it? No. I wouldn't do that to him. Even though a part of me wants to," he added with bitter honesty.

"Neither would I," Nicole admitted glumly.

Shoving aside a pile of clothing, she sank onto the side of the bed.

"So what are you going to do now?" he asked as he watched her prop her chin on her fist.

What could she do? Nicole wondered wildly. He had control of her money. And if she didn't stay put, Belle Rouge would go to the state. "What the hell can I do?"

He shrugged as though it was all her decision, but Nicole knew he wouldn't give up this place without a fight. The only thing she wasn't certain about was whether he wanted it for the financial gain or because it had been his home.

"Look, Nicole, I'm not the one who arranged all this. So don't look at me as if you'd like to run a knife blade through me."

"You're a smart businessman, Logan. Surely you can come up with some sort of alternative to this—" she gestured helplessly "—this situation we're in."

He came to stand in front of her, and Nicole tilted her head to look up at him. As Logan gazed down at her ripe lips and lowered lashes, the thought of Belle Rouge was lost in the desire to toss her among the piles of clothes and teach her what it was like to make love to a man. To him.

"There's nothing I can do. And if you think we can just pretend to live here, think again. Dad's lawyer is going to have someone checking. And often."

She closed her eyes as the enormity of it washed over her like a suffocating wave of saltwater. "It's so hard to believe Lyle could be this conniving."

"Or generous," he added caustically. "Don't forget that. Remember, you believed you were getting nothing."

She opened her eyes and her heart gave a hard jolt. The subtle glint in his gray eyes told her his thoughts weren't totally absorbed with Belle Rouge business. And she wondered if he was recalling last night when he'd kissed her. Or had the incident been so mundane to him he'd instantly forgotten it?

"I haven't received anything yet," she replied curtly, while trying to hold on to her scattered senses. Even if he was remembering their kiss, she had to forget it, she told herself.

"But you will. If you stay put."

She sighed. "For the next six months? With you? I don't think that's possible. Besides, in that length of time, I might decide I want to get married."

Logan inwardly winced, then jammed his hands into the front pockets of his jeans. "For the past few days I've been thinking all this over, Nicole. And I believe I've come up with a solution to all our problems."

Sudden hope lit her face. "You have? Why haven't you suggested it before now?"

"Because I wanted you to hear all the stipulations of the will first."

When he failed to go on, Nicole's expression grew wary. "Why?"

"So you'll understand my suggestion is the only logical conclusion."

"You're beginning to make it sound dreadful," she said.

He grimaced. "I'm sure you'll see it that way."

Something in his face made her heart begin to pound. "Why? What do you think we should do?"

His cool gray gaze met hers. "Get married. To each other."

Chapter Three

Nicole was suddenly on her feet, her expression incredulous. "Have you totally lost your mind? We hate each other!"

One corner of his mouth lifted mockingly. "Last night you didn't exactly act as though you hated me."

"Last night I wasn't myself!" Nicole started past him, but his hand gripped her shoulder.

"Nicole, you need to know that episode beneath the live oak has nothing to do with us getting married."

Refusing to look at him, she said curtly, "There's no way in hell I'd marry you."

"Not even to save Belle Rouge?" he asked softly.

Her gaze fluttered up to his face. The regret she saw in his dark features filled her with an odd sense of confusion. It shouldn't matter to her if she disappointed him or caused him anguish. But for some idiotic reason it did.

"I can't believe you want this place that badly."

His eyes scanned the soft lines and angles of her face. "It's my home."

"You haven't been here in four years," she reminded him, then added sardonically, "But then I should know sentimentality isn't behind your need for Belle Rouge. It's the monetary value."

His nostrils flared as he continued to gaze down at her. "Why I want to keep Belle Rouge is my own business. But as for the worth of the place, you'd be a damn fool to lose it all just because you think you don't like me."

"Money isn't everything."

His gray eyes swept slowly up and down the length of her. "No. I guess it isn't."

Her body began to burn in spite of her effort to remain indifferent to him. "You're asking me to sell my body. My pride and self-respect."

"I'm not asking you to sell anything. This will be a marriage of convenience only. After the six months pass, you can divorce me and go on your merry way. Belle Rouge will be mine and you'll have all the money you need to live on."

He made it sound so logical, practical and cold, it was all Nicole could do to keep from outwardly shivering. "You mean if I became your wife, after six months time I could legally sign over my two quarters of the plantation to you?"

"Yes. And in return I'd give you the market value for your shares. What could be wrong with that?"

Nothing. If he wasn't Logan. But he'd insulted and hurt her mother and for the past ten years practically forsaken his father. How could Nicole dismiss all the pain he'd caused her loved ones? Even more, how could she forget about last night and the way he'd kissed her? The way she'd kissed him?

"I can't give you an answer right now. I'll have to think about it."

At that moment, Logan realized he was still holding on to her shoulder. Yet he didn't drop his hand. It was as though his body deliberately refused to deny itself the pleasure of touching her warm flesh.

"Why? What is there to think about?"

"I don't know about you, Logan, but I consider marriage a serious step to take. And I'm not so sure we could exist under the same roof together. Especially after the way we…kissed each other."

He groaned. "I told you that has nothing to do with our getting married. Don't worry about it happening again. I won't let it."

"Is that what you want?"

Surprise arched his brows, then his eyelids lowered to the moist curve of her lips. "Yes. No. Damn it," he muttered thickly. Then before he could stop it, his hand deserted her shoulder to glide up the side of her smooth neck.

Nicole's brown eyes darkened, then widened in shock as his fingers curled around her nape and gently urged her toward him. "Logan?"

The whisper of his name seemed to snap the blank, hypnotic look from his eyes, and suddenly, without warning, his hand fell away and he turned on his heel and headed toward the door.

"I'll send Darcy up to help you get your room back in order," he said gruffly. Before Nicole could make any sort of reply, he stepped into the hallway.

By the time the door closed behind him, her legs were shaking weakly and her heart was pounding wildly. Logan wanted to make her his wife. In name only. Yet just a few seconds ago, she could have sworn making love to her was what he wanted the most.

What did it all mean? What could it mean? she wondered wildly. Although they'd never lived as a family, Logan was her stepbrother. She couldn't think of him as her husband! Yet it was all she could do to stop herself from running after him and begging him to kiss her one more time.

But she had to remember Logan was a McNally and she was a Carrington. One union between the two families had already wreaked havoc. Another one would surely destroy Belle Rouge and eventually the both of them.

"I'm sorry, Miss Carrington, but as the executor of Lyle's will, it's my duty to see everything is carried through as he wished. I can't change his instructions, even though I do understand what a difficult situation this whole thing puts you in."

Nicole wanted to scream at the smiling, middle-aged lawyer sitting behind the wide polished desk. He had no idea what a difficult situation she was in. And if the truth was known he probably didn't give a damn, so long as he got his allotted fee.

"Well, I'll be honest with you, Mr. Thorndyke," Nicole told him. "If it wasn't for Belle Rouge going to the state I would have packed up and left a week ago."

His smile suddenly vanished. "I'm certain the old man was counting on your love for the place to hold you there. And when you think about it, Miss Carrington, it isn't asking too much of you. Just think of all you'll be getting in return. As I understand, the yearly sale of the cane crop alone is very profitable. So is the pecan crop. And though I realize the house needs a bit of face-lifting here and there, its value on the real estate market would be quite staggering. All in all, your inheritance is not something you should take lightly.''

Nicole understood the money value involved. But she wanted to tell this man there were some things worth more than money. Like her pride, self-respect and, most of all, her peace of mind.

For the past week, since Logan had suggested they marry to solve their problem, Nicole had carefully avoided the man, staying mostly in her bedroom or outside the house. Yet even that didn't spare her the evening meals when he sat across from her and made stilted conversation, while she wondered how much longer it would be before he pressed her for an answer to his proposal.

Deciding she'd wasted enough time in the stuffy law office, she reached for her purse and rose to her feet. "Believe me, I'm not taking anything about this lightly, Mr. Thorndyke.''

The lawyer politely stood and walked her to the door. "I'm glad to hear it. I would hate for you to lose your interest in the place. As I'm sure Mr. McNally would hate to lose his. And when I discussed this whole thing with him a few days ago, he seemed to be very concerned about your needs.''

Nicole could hardly imagine it. Logan had always thought about his own needs and to hell with everybody else.

"Of course he would be concerned," Nicole retorted. "He knows if I'm not happy, he's not happy.''

The lawyer's brows lifted and he cleared his throat as if to say he wasn't ready to argue that point. "Well, if there's anything else I can do for you, Miss Carrington, please don't hesitate to call.''

The man had already made it clear he could do nothing about the will. But he'd been Belle Rouge's legal advisor for years, not to mention a dear friend of Lyle's, so she didn't want to insult him.

''Thank you, Mr. Thorndyke, for taking the time to explain the situation. If I have any more questions I'll contact you.'' She shook his hand, then walked out of the law office and into the muggy afternoon.

Once she'd started her car and pulled out onto the busy street of downtown Natchitoches, she headed toward a route that would lead her to Highway One and eventually Belle Rouge. But at the last minute she changed her mind, turned toward the river and didn't stop until she reached a quiet residential street.

The temperature was in the high nineties, with a humidity to match. Nicole greatly appreciated the deep shade of the century-old magnolias as she stepped up to the door of the well-kept antebellum home and lifted the heavy knocker.

Moments later, a tall brunette in her early forties opened the door, then quickly let out a squeal of delight. ''Nicole! What a pleasant surprise! Come in.''

She swung the oak door even wider while Nicole hesitated on the threshold. ''Were you busy, Amelia? I don't want to interrupt anything.''

Her soft laugh tinkled like happy music. ''Don't be ridiculous. I'm never too busy for you. Besides, I didn't have to work today. I'm being horribly lazy.''

Amelia was a physical therapist at a local hospital. Nicole had first met her more than two years ago, when Simone had suffered her first stroke. Amelia's gentle but stern tactics had allowed her mother to recover enough mobility to enjoy the last two years of her life. Since then Nicole had become fast and loyal friends with the woman.

"I can't stay long," Nicole promised as she stepped into the house and followed her through a parlor and down a long hallway. "Darcy will be worried if I'm not home in time for supper."

As they walked, Amelia said over her shoulder, "Surely you have time for iced tea. I just made a fresh pitcher. Let's have some out on the veranda," she suggested.

"Sounds nice," Nicole agreed. The hour she'd spent in Thorndyke's office had drained her both physically and mentally. She'd desperately hoped the lawyer could find some loophole to allow her and Logan to go their separate ways. Now she had to face the fact that she was stuck with him for at least six months.

"What brings you into town today?" Amelia asked. "I'm surprised to see you."

"I've been talking to a lawyer," Nicole replied glumly.

The other woman pulled a tall glass pitcher from the refrigerator. "Tying up loose ends with your mother's estate?"

Nicole shook her head. "No. Mother didn't really have much to leave other than her car and a small savings account. Everything else belonged to Lyle. There's…other problems I was seeing him about."

"Well, I hate that you're having other problems, but I'm glad to see you're out and about and not burying yourself at Belle Rouge."

"I don't bury myself at Belle Rouge. It's my home and I love it there." Or at least she did love it there, she thought miserably, before Logan moved in and took control.

Amelia frowned as she picked up a tray loaded with the pitcher of tea, glasses and a small plate of cookies. "Yes, I know. But I wish..." She stopped and motioned for Nicole to precede her through a door leading to a screened-in porch.

"You wish I was living here in Natchitoches," Nicole finished as she sank onto a chaise longue.

Amelia took a seat on the one next to hers and began to pour the tea. After she'd handed a glass to Nicole, she said, "I would enjoy having you live closer. You know you're just like a daughter to me. But I'd be happy for you to live anywhere except where you are. It's too isolated. You're just not getting—"

"The social contact I need," Nicole finished for her. She smiled faintly as she added, "You ought to know by now that I'm not much for the social life."

Amelia gave her a long, pointed look. "Your life has been tied up with caring for your mother. Have you been thinking about what you're going to do with yourself now that she's gone?"

Nicole sighed. "Not really."

Amelia shot her an odd look. "Why not? Simone wouldn't want you to be just sitting around grieving."

Nicole absently rubbed her finger over the cold, sapphire-blue glass she was holding. "I know that. And I'm not."

Amelia nodded with approval. "Good. You've worked so hard to get your accounting degree. Now you can finally put it to use."

It was true she'd worked hard to get through college. Then, just as she'd entered her junior year and the dream of becoming an accountant was finally drawing closer, her mother had been stricken with a stroke. Out of love, Nicole had chosen to stay home and care for her.

"Maybe I can eventually," she told the other woman. "Right now…things are up in the air."

Amelia looked at her with concern. "Up in the air? Don't you have people running the plantation for you? What could be holding you back now?"

Nicole shook her head, then sighed. Maybe she should tell Amelia the whole situation, she thought.

"All the workers have stayed on. That's not the problem. There have been some major changes at Belle Rouge since I've last seen you."

Amelia suddenly laughed, and as Nicole glanced over at her, she thought how wonderful it would be to be so beautiful and confident. Even though the woman had a failed marriage behind her, and she'd been treated badly by a man, she wasn't overly mistrustful of the opposite sex, the way Nicole was.

"Changes?" Amelia asked with humor. "The plantation was built in the late 1700s and the only thing different now is it has indoor bathrooms and telephones."

"Well," Nicole answered, "outwardly the place hasn't changed. But—" she stopped and swallowed a long drink of tea while Amelia waited for her to continue "—do you remember I have a stepbrother?"

Her features suddenly wrinkled with concentration. "Vaguely. I recall you mentioning something about him living in Shreveport and never coming home to Belle Rouge."

"That's right. The day Mother and I moved in, Logan moved out. He never wanted us in his family. But now—now I have to live with the man!"

This news brought Amelia upright in her seat. "Live with him? You mean your stepbrother has moved back home?"

Nicole nodded stiffly. "And he intends to stay. Permanently."

The other woman studied Nicole's miserable expression. "Obviously you don't like him."

Like Logan? The meek emotion couldn't begin to describe what she felt for the man. It was becoming apparent as each day went by that she didn't know if she loved him, hated him or wanted to kill him. Perhaps all three.

"Amelia, the man has always blamed my mother for breaking up his parents' marriage. He believes his mother died because my mother caused her to turn into an alcoholic."

"Sounds like your stepbrother is a real darling. How old is he?"

"Thirty-four."

"Then he has a wife and family?"

Nicole shook her head, while thinking how different things might be if Logan had a wife. At least then he couldn't have asked her to marry him. Nor would he have kissed her senseless.

"Logan has never been married. I really don't think he's the marrying kind."

Amelia's brows lifted with new speculation. "Exactly what kind is he?"

Nicole grimaced. "Dark. Tall and lean. He's a handsome man. But the inside ruins the outside, if you know what I mean."

Amelia laughed knowingly. "Oh, yes, honey. I was married to one of those. Nowadays just give me an ugly man with a big heart."

Nicole sighed. "Anyway, to my surprise, I own part of Belle Rouge now. So...I'm not sure how that's going to affect my plans to find an accounting job."

Amelia clucked her tongue. "I know you love Belle Rouge. And I can certainly appreciate its beauty and its significance to our state's history. But I think you ought to sell your part to your stepbrother and get a place of your own. You need to be dating young men and enjoying life. All you've done so far is go to school and care for your mother."

"That's all I was interested in doing," Nicole said dourly.

"I know. But you should have enjoyed yourself along the way."

Nicole frowned as she lifted the tea glass to her lips. "And wound up like my mother? Pregnant and alone?"

"You can't forget that, can you? That some man didn't care enough about either of you to stick around?"

Nicole looked beyond the wire screen to a spot in the yard where red, white and pink roses covered an arched trellis. Yet she wasn't really seeing their beauty, she was remembering back to a time when she was a very small girl, sitting on the floor of the diner's kitchen playing with her dolls while her mother waited tables out front. She'd pretend and imagine that her father would come and take them away to a beautiful place. But it never happened. She'd never once seen his face. And after all these years she never wanted to.

"I've tried, Amelia. I can't." She glanced back at her friend. "Only last week Logan reminded me I was an illegitimate child born out of wedlock and never belonged at Belle Rouge."

Amelia let out an unladylike snort. "He sounds more charming by the minute."

"Oh, believe me, he can be very charming." Especially if he took you in his arms and kissed you until you couldn't breathe, Nicole thought. "But Logan is beside the point. So far I've not met a man who wanted more from me than sex."

Amelia shook her head as she reached for a sugar cookie. "That's because you haven't let yourself meet the right one. You're letting that whole thing with what's-his-name…"

"Bryce. How could you forget? I certainly haven't."

The other woman sighed with frustration. "Well, you should have forgotten. Long ago. Do you think you're the only young girl who was ever duped with sweet promises from a man? There are thousands out there who've gone through the same thing you have." Amelia added, "What you need to do now is focus on your future."

Nicole sighed. "That's hard to do when my hands are going to be tied for the next six months."

"What happens in six months?"

Nicole didn't want to get into the whole thing with Amelia now. Without discussing it, she knew the other woman would be shocked if she told her about Logan's proposal. "For one thing, my share of Belle Rouge will be official."

Amelia regarded her for a long moment. "And I can see how important that is to you. I wish it weren't. But it is. And maybe that's good. Because I have a feeling you'll never be happy away from Belle Rouge."

Nicole glanced hopelessly at her friend. "I think you're right, Amelia. And that's what scares me the very most."

Chapter Four

When Nicole's car came speeding up the long oak
alley leading to the house, Logan was sitting on the
front porch, sipping Coke laced with Kentucky bourbon. The past few days had been dry and the dirt road
had once again grown dusty. The dust followed the
dark blue car like a gray plume until the vehicle halted
abruptly in front of the white picket fence.

Logan didn't want to acknowledge the relief he felt
at seeing her back home, yet he felt it anyway. And as
he watched her leave the car and slowly climb the wide
staircase leading up to the porch, he was momentarily
captured by the beautiful image she made in her simple
flowered dress and wide-brimmed straw hat.

Nicole was about to go into the house when she
spotted Logan sitting in a willow chair at the end of
the porch. His jeans and boots were dusty, but his white
T-shirt looked clean and fresh. She wondered what
he'd been doing all day. From the looks of his clothing
he'd been in the cane fields. Yet she wouldn't ask. Not

for a minute did she want to let him think she was interested.

After a moment's hesitation, she walked over to him. Sally, her bluetick hound, was lying at his feet. Nicole squatted down and scratched the lazy dog between the ears, then glanced at Logan.

"What are you doing?" she asked bluntly.

"Waiting on you." *To tell me you'll marry me,* he silently added.

Her brows lifted. "Why?"

He frowned as though her question was the height of stupidity. "For supper. Why else?"

She tried not to looked surprised even though she was. She'd never expected Logan to consider her in his daily routine. Rising to her full height again, she said, "You didn't have to wait on me."

"I could hardly enjoy eating with you out gallivanting to heaven only knows where," he said accusingly.

She swept off her hat and pushed her hand through her loose hair. Logan watched the silky, red-gold strands slide through her fingers, then fall against her slender white neck. When she'd left the house this morning, he'd been down at the workshed talking to Leo, Belle Rouge's farm manager. Logan hadn't known where she'd gone, and all afternoon he'd found himself wondering what she was doing, and listening for her return.

"Darcy knew where I went. All you had to do was ask her."

He snorted. "Why should I have to ask the hired help where my stepsister has gone off to? You should have had the decency to tell me yourself. You've been gone all day!"

Nicole quivered with anger as she watched him lift

the squatty tumbler to his lips. "Darcy is not the hired help!"

"I beg your pardon, I just signed her paycheck this morning."

"You know exactly what I mean. She's been in this family for years!" Her eyes narrowed as they cut a path over his dark features. "But I keep forgetting you were never around. She couldn't feel like family to you. But then, who could?"

She turned on her heel and headed into the house. With one graceful lunge, Logan was out of the chair and right behind her. Behind them, Sally lifted her head and whined at the prospect of being left alone.

"What is that supposed to mean?" Logan snapped.

Inside the parlor, Nicole tossed her hat onto a settee, then headed on down the hallway to the kitchen. "You don't know how to belong to a family. Nor do you want to."

"Oh, well, now isn't that rich coming from you," he drawled sarcastically. "I used to care a damn lot. Until you and your mother came along and tore my family asunder!"

"So you say," she said with disgust. "The way I see it, your family was torn long before me or my mother ever came into the picture."

"If it eases your conscience to believe such a thing, then go ahead."

From the corner of her eye, Nicole watched him toss back the last of his drink as she washed her hands at the kitchen sink. He was obviously out of sorts with her for being gone all day, although she didn't understand why that had ruffled his feathers. He rarely spoke more than ten words a day to her. This evening was definitely an exception.

"Just how many drinks have you had?" she asked.

"One. Why? You think I have to be drunk to tell the truth? Or are you afraid I'll turn into an alcoholic? It's in my genes, remember?"

Ignoring his sarcastic glare, she walked over to the gas range and opened the oven, where Darcy had left several dishes under a low heat.

"You're really quite a peach this evening, aren't you?" she said.

"My mood was fine until I had to sit around for more than an hour, starving."

"I told you there was no need for you to wait on me. You could have eaten anytime you wanted to."

That was the hell of it, Logan thought. He was well aware he could have walked into the kitchen anytime and filled his plate. And yet he'd been loath to do so. During the past week, the evening meal was the only time Nicole bothered to come around him. This evening he'd had to admit the awful realization that he'd grown used to sharing supper with her and didn't want to eat without her sitting across the table from him.

"Darcy was worried about you," he muttered, changing the subject. "She said you'd planned to be back by five."

"I stopped by a friend's before I left town."

With hands protected by quilted mittens, she carried a platter of ham to the small table, then went back for the accompanying vegetables. All the while Logan watched her movements as keenly as Sally would watch a squirrel hopping from tree to tree.

"A male friend, I suppose."

His comment bewildered her. He couldn't really care who her friends were, Nicole told herself. Unless he thought it would ultimately affect him.

"What difference would it make if I'd been seeing a man? You can't choose my friends. And if I want to get married, there's nothing you can do about it."

The reality of her statement hit him hard, even though he knew he was crazy to let it. "So you were seeing a man," he said tightly.

She motioned toward the table. "Everything is ready but the drinks. Do you want another bourbon or do you think you can stomach my company on a plain glass of well water?"

He jerked out the chair she normally sat in and gestured for her to sit. "I'll get the drinks. You tell me about the man."

For a moment Nicole had the wild inclination to fabricate a boyfriend just to see his reaction. But she was too honest to do such a thing. And besides, she mentally argued with herself, Logan's opinion didn't mean anything to her.

"What's the matter, Logan? Afraid some man will marry me and you'll end up losing half of Belle Rouge? What are you going to do? Keep me chained here and run off every male visitor that happens to drive up the lane?"

Logan wished his inheritance was the only reason he felt so possessive of Nicole. But since that night he'd learned she was a virgin he'd been torn between wanting to protect her, and coveting her. It was crazy and yet he couldn't seem to control himself.

"If I have to. You're too young to think about a serious relationship."

"But I'm not too young to be your wife," she reminded him ironically.

"I told you. That would only be a union on paper. Nothing else," he said curtly.

Nothing else, Nicole repeated to herself as her gaze traveled up and down his hard, lean body. Why did it feel like it would be so much more?

He carried two tall glasses of ice water to the table and took the seat opposite her. "You don't realize the sort of problems a man can get you into," he stated, "and I'm talking about more than getting you pregnant."

Her face flamed with heat. "What could be worse?"

"Marrying you under false pretenses for your money. Don't you think that would be far worse?"

"I'd like to think I'm a better judge of character than that," she muttered. But was she? Nicole asked herself. Bryce had certainly fooled her for a time. And the other night when Logan had kissed her, maybe he'd done it thinking he could entice her into marrying him.

But no, she quickly argued with herself. He'd lose Belle Rouge and the fortune that went along with it before he'd ever pretend to love her, a Carrington. No, he'd kissed her out of anger. And that was the only reason.

"Men are adept at lying," he said. "It's just part of our makeup. Especially when it comes to women. You should know that, Nicole."

If Nicole knew anything about men, she knew they were born to charm and lie and desert. Along with her unknown father, Bryce had taught her a good lesson. But she wasn't going to share that humiliating experience with Logan. He already thought she was too naive to take care of herself.

"Well, for what it's worth, the friend I visited today wasn't a man. Although I did see a man today. Mr. Thorndyke."

Logan's fork paused in midair. "You went to see Dad's executor?"

She nodded. "You'll be relieved to know he isn't willing to cut me any slack."

"Did you honestly think he would?"

Nicole shrugged. "He's a man, isn't he? You just told me how deceitful your gender is. There was a chance he might have offered me some sort of deal. Especially if I could have convinced him it would be worth his while."

Logan's expression was suddenly thunderous. "What did you do, tell him you'd sleep with him if he'd change a few lines in the will?"

Her food forgotten, she flung down her fork. "Is that what you really think of me?"

"Like mother, like daughter."

She lunged from her chair, but Logan instantly reached out and grabbed her wrist.

"Sit down!" he warned.

"Not with you."

She expected him to jerk her back into the chair and was shocked when instead he stood up to face her.

"Don't be childish," he muttered fiercely.

Her nostrils flared as her brown eyes raked over his hard features. She didn't know how anyone could look so good on the outside and be so monstrous on the inside.

"It would be childish of me to continue to sit here and take your nasty remarks. No, thank you. I'll eat later."

"You'll eat now!"

She tried to jerk away from his grasp, but he held her wrist fast in his grip. "You're not in any position to order me around, Logan!"

Her breasts were heaving with anger and exertion. Logan's gaze instinctively dropped to their fullness beneath the pale pink fabric of her dress. "You think I'm going to sit back and let you make a fool of yourself and my family name?"

"I wasn't making a fool of anyone, including myself!" she snapped.

"Oh no?" His eyes fell farther down, to where the slit at the side of her skirt revealed part of her shapely calf. "What do you think that old man was thinking when he was looking at your bare leg?"

"He wasn't—"

Logan snatched her chin and jerked her face close to his. "More than likely he was wondering if you were wearing panties, and just how long it would take him to get into them."

Instantly, her free hand shot up and her palm cracked against his jaw. "You're filthy! And I—"

"You don't know what I am! But if you want a man, you don't have to go running off to town to find one," he muttered through clenched jaws. Then, blindly, he jerked her forward and into his arms.

Nicole struggled but she couldn't avoid his mouth as it clamped down over hers. As his lips made a rough foray, his hands caught her by the waist and he slowly inched her backward.

Eventually her hips bumped into the cabinets, where he bent her back over the counter. A plastic glass clattered to the floor and some sort of liquid splashed her ankles, while on the counter her elbow sank into something mushy. The fleeting thought that it was meringue pie flashed through her mind, but the mess on her arm was nothing compared to the wild need to escape his punishing embrace.

His tongue was thrust between her teeth and his hand was on her bare thigh, sliding ever higher. She knew she had to stop him before her body decided to surrender and they both did something they would later regret.

With every ounce of strength she could muster, Nicole shoved against his chest. The unexpected movement caused his hold on her to slacken. Instantly, she ripped away from him and bolted for the back door.

By the time she reached the gazebo, she was sobbing openly. While she tried to dash the tears from her blurred eyes, she heard Logan's footsteps behind her.

Keeping her back to him, she warned, "Don't come near me!"

"Nicole! I'm not going to hurt you," he said in a pained voice.

When she didn't respond, he carefully moved closer and took her by the shoulders. "I'm sorry, Nicole. I'm sorry." His head bent and he pressed his lips against her ear. "I've never acted that way with any woman."

She whirled around to face him, and her tortured eyes roamed his face for some sort of answers. "I wasn't afraid you were going to hurt me, Logan. But you were angry and—"

"The idea of you teasing Thorndyke was..." He stopped and with an agonized groan cupped his hands around her face. "I didn't like it."

"I wasn't teasing Thorndyke," she said with a sniff.

"I know. I just—hell, Nicole, I don't want to think of any man putting his hands on you!"

"Logan!"

His name came out as a stunned gasp, and Logan's lips twisted with self-contempt.

"Go ahead and tell me how damn stupid that is. I

already know it. And I know it's got to stop. But right
now…''

He didn't go on, and Nicole watched in stunned fas-
cination as his lips drew nearer to hers until finally he
was kissing her, really kissing her. And as she opened
her mouth to him and wound her arms around his neck,
she knew she was in deep trouble. Because she feared
it was more than her body that wanted him now. Her
heart wanted him, too.

Logan's mind was tumbling, falling into the sweetness of her mouth, the velvet band of her arms clinging
to his neck, the soft heat of her body pressed against
his.

He wasn't supposed to be kissing her, holding her,
wanting her. But she was like forbidden fruit to a
starved man. He had to have his fill no matter the consequences.

His arms tightened around her, his mouth grew
greedy and moments turned to minutes. Then suddenly,
from somewhere at the edge of his foggy brain, he
recognized the sound of a motor at the front of the
house, then the slamming of a car door.

With a reluctant groan, he ripped his mouth from
hers and forced himself to take a step back. "Someone
just drove up," he whispered thickly. "I'd better go
see who it is."

Somehow Nicole managed to nod at him, and he
turned and hurried out of the garden. Once he was out
of sight, she sank down onto the steps of the gazebo
and tried to gather herself together.

Her hands were shaking and her cheeks were on fire.
There was an ache deep inside her and her breath was
still coming in rapid gulps. Everything had happened
like a whirlwind. One minute the two of them had been

arguing, and the next thing she knew she was back in his arms, and kissing him was all that mattered.

What was she going to do? She wasn't supposed to want Logan. He'd never had one iota of respect for her. He'd never thought her good enough to live on Belle Rouge. Yet none of that seemed to matter whenever she was near him.

With a frantic little groan, she thrust her fingers through her hair, scraping the tips against her scalp as she lifted her face skyward. Of all the men she'd encountered through college and since, none of them came remotely close to affecting her the way Logan did. When he touched her, she lost all common sense!

How could she marry him? In no time at all, she'd wind up in his bed. The idea brought a mocking twist to her lips. She could have very well ended up making love to him a few minutes ago. Without the sanctity of marriage. And the last thing she wanted to do was end up like her mother. Raising a child alone. Deserted by a man she believed had loved her.

No, she told herself desperately. Whether she married Logan or not, she had to get a grip on herself. She couldn't give her body or her heart to the man. There was no doubt in her mind that he'd surely trample them both.

Minutes later on the front porch, Logan watched Leo drive away before he glanced to his left. Night was falling and shadows gathered under the live oaks to shroud the house and grounds with darkness. Logan couldn't see whether Nicole was still in the garden. And he sure as hell wasn't about to go check.

It was a good thing the foreman had chosen this evening to speak with him about a problem with one of the tractors. Without the interruption, Logan didn't know if he could have stopped himself from carrying Nicole into the house and making love to her.

The idea left him shocked and shaken. She was his stepsister, and a virgin at that! How could he want her so? He'd known plenty of women through the years and he'd suffered through just as many bouts of lust. Yet none of those women or those urgings had come close to what he experienced when he was near Nicole.

What in hell was he going to do if, by some miracle, she agreed to marry him? he wondered. He'd already insisted the union would be in name only. And in the same breath he'd promised he could keep his hands off her. But it hadn't taken him long to break that promise, he thought ruefully. So married or not, how did he expect to keep his hands off her for the next six months?

As he turned and stepped into the house, he told himself he had to get over this crazy attraction. Because there was no way he was going to let his body or his heart become dependent on Nicole. Belle Rouge was all he wanted. The plantation was the only reason he'd come back and it was the only reason he would stay.

The next morning Nicole stayed in her bedroom until she felt she'd given Logan enough time to have his breakfast and leave the house.

After the past week, she was beginning to learn his routine. Mornings he usually spent down at the fields, afternoons in the study, where he tended to the business end of the plantation.

For the most part since Lyle had died, the plantation had simply gone on running itself. The hired hands had continued to look after the crops and the grounds, while

Lyle's lawyers had signed the paychecks and tended to all the business and legal decisions. Nicole had taken care of the bookkeeping, but she or her mother had not had any say about expenditures or profits or the crops themselves. And as far as she knew, Logan hadn't, either. Until now.

She didn't know why Lyle hadn't made his son the legal supervisor of Belle Rouge once he'd passed on. But then maybe he had, and Logan had refused the job because Simone was still living here. It wouldn't surprise Nicole if that was the case. Logan had never tried to hide his feelings toward his stepmother. But whatever the reason, things had definitely changed. Logan was in control now.

In more ways than one, she thought with self-disgust as she headed down the staircase. But that was going to change, too. After their passionate tryst in the garden last night, she'd done a lot of long, hard thinking, and she'd decided she was going to remain cool and indifferent to the man. No matter what it cost her.

"Good morning, Nicole."

On the bottom step, she turned to see him descending the stairs behind her. His dark hair was wet and combed back from his face. A gray chambray work shirt was rolled to his elbows and tucked into the waist of a pair of faded jeans, yet the inexpensive garment couldn't camouflage his proud breeding. No matter where he was or what he was doing, he would always be a McNally. Rich, powerful and devastatingly handsome.

She let out a long breath as her hand gripped the balustrade. "Good morning, Logan."

He stopped his descent one step above her. The faint scent of his spicy cologne touched her nostrils as her gaze drifted over the sharp angles of his face, the strong brown column of his throat, then back to his eyes. The gray shirt emphasized their cool color, and for a moment she felt trapped by the intensity of his stare.

"You're late coming down this morning," he said. "Are you feeling ill?"

Heat seeped to the surface of her cheeks. It wasn't like him to be concerned about her well-being, and while he continued to study her closely, she wondered if he really was, or if this was just a game he'd decided to play with her.

"No. I'm fine. I was just about to have breakfast."

"Then I'll wait," he said.

Her brows lifted. "For what?"

"For you to eat. I'd like for you to ride down to the cane fields with me."

Her expression turned a little more than wary, making Logan frown.

"Why?"

"Because I want to talk with you."

She glanced away from him as memories began to attack her from all directions. The feel of his arms around her, his hard mouth crushing down on hers, his hand sliding up her thigh. She'd not wanted any of it to end. Not really. And she wondered if Logan had felt the extent of her desire.

"We can talk here." To Nicole's dismay her voice had turned husky. She cleared her throat and forced herself to glance at him. His arms were folded against his chest and a frown puckered his forehead. "There's no need to go to the cane fields."

"I realize that. But it's been a few days since I looked at the crops. And I don't want us to be interrupted. By anything."

Her eyes widened. "Look, Logan, I'm not about to repeat last night! If that's what you're thinking—"

The rest of her words were chopped off as his hand suddenly clamped down on her shoulder. "Listen, Nicole, if I wanted to seduce you I wouldn't have to take you to the cane fields to do it!"

She swallowed as the warmth of his fingers drove home the truth of his words. Not to go with him would be childish on her part, and that was the last impression she wanted him to have of her.

Squaring her shoulders, she turned and tilted up her chin. "All right, Logan. Give me a few minutes for breakfast and I'll join you," she said.

His eyes gleamed with approval. "Good. Meet me on the front porch in twenty minutes."

In the kitchen, Nicole took her time eating grits and ham and drinking a large mug of coffee before she finally headed to the front of the house to meet Logan.

When she pushed through the screen door, she found him leaning against one of the tall white pillars. A coffee cup was in his hand and Sally was sitting at his heels. He looked so at home, it was hard for Nicole to remember he'd forsaken this place for ten years.

Logan's gaze skimmed over the picture she made in her full gauze skirt and matching tank top, then settled back on her face. "Ready?"

She nodded and he tossed away the last few swallows in his cup, then pushed away from the pillar.

Nicole followed him down the steps and out to the navy-blue pickup waiting in the drive. Sally jumped up on the open tailgate as though she'd already been invited to go and since Logan didn't object, Nicole allowed the dog to remain in the back of the vehicle.

After he helped Nicole into the passenger seat, Logan headed the truck down the lane and away from the house. The canopy made by the live oaks blocked out the morning sun, but when they merged onto the highway, it blazed brightly over the flat bottomland.

"It's going to be hot today," Logan commented as he watched her squint against the sunlight.

As far as Nicole was concerned it was already too hot the moment she'd climbed into his pickup. "Just right for growing cane."

"Lots of people would label us crazy for living in this climate."

She glanced at him. "I wouldn't live anywhere else."

He didn't know if she was speaking of Belle Rouge or the South in general. And he wasn't going to ask. He had too much to say to her and he wanted to keep things in order. The same way he'd tried to keep his life. On schedule, without any surprises or deviation of plans.

Logan hadn't necessarily set out to be that rigid sort of man. At one time, he'd been more like his father, who'd been impulsive and had lived life to the fullest. But after Tracie had duped and deceived him, Logan had learned not to give in to impulses or desires. He'd kept his mind on his job at Louisiana State University. And if he got to wanting female companionship, he kept the encounters short and temporary.

A couple of miles down the highway, Logan turned onto a dirt road that ran along the edge of one of the bigger fields of Belle Rouge. The access road stretched all the way to the river, which was lined with oaks and willows and wild magnolia trees.

Logan stopped beneath the shade of an oak and killed the motor. Nicole looked over at him as he pushed a button on the armrest and lowered both windows.

"I don't understand why you had to bring me all the way out here to talk to me. If you were afraid of Darcy hearing something—"

"Darcy hears everything," he interrupted.

Nicole frowned. "You don't like her," she accused.

He shook his head. "I didn't say that. But now that you brought it up, it's Darcy who doesn't like me. She thinks of me as a Yankee. An enemy that's invaded her territory. Just like you do," he added.

Nicole sighed. "That's not what this is all about, is it? I'm not in the mood to start hashing it out with you before my breakfast even has time to digest."

"At this point I don't care what you think of me. Someday you might understand how I felt back then and why I stayed away. But I'm not going to count on it."

There was no anger or sarcasm in his voice, and Nicole suddenly got the impression she was looking at a different Logan. Or maybe she'd never really known this man, after all.

He gestured toward the windshield and out to the acres and acres of thick green cane. "The plants look good. If the weather doesn't give us any surprises before harvesttime, Belle Rouge will profit."

"It's beautiful," Nicole said wistfully.

"I've never seen anyplace more beautiful," he agreed.

Her eyes left the crop to settle on his face. "I think you really mean that," she said softly.

His lips twisted in a sardonic line. "Why should that surprise you?"

She shrugged. "Why shouldn't it? In the years since

I've been here, you haven't exactly shown an interest in this place. I really didn't think you cared about it."

He drew in a long breath and let it out. "I cared."

She turned in the seat to face him. "Then why didn't you come back and oversee things after your father died?"

"I couldn't."

Her eyes slowly searched his closed face. "Why?" she asked bluntly. "Because my mother was still living here?"

He sighed. "Yes. But not for the reason you're thinking."

Nicole closed her eyes and tilted her head back in resignation. "I suppose you have a good reason?"

The sarcasm in her voice sliced through him, though he didn't know why. He wasn't the villain here. He never had been.

"Because I didn't want to make your mother's life here awkward."

Nicole's eyes popped open and she stared at him. "I can't believe you have the gall to say such a thing! You never wanted my mother to have a life here, period. Much less an awkward one."

He groaned softly. "That was when I was very young, Nicole. Before our parents married. By the time Dad died, I'd gotten past the bad feelings I'd harbored toward Simone."

She looked at him skeptically. "That's not the way it looked to me. After Lyle's funeral, you never came back."

"I kept in contact with Thorndyke's office to make sure everything was going smoothly up here. But as for moving back here to live, I realized I had once hurt your mother badly by offering her that money to leave town and my father. I figured even if I apologized to her, she'd still resent my being here.''

''Mother wasn't like that. She was a very forgiving person. In fact, she told me a long time ago that she'd forgiven you and that I...should, too.''

He rubbed a hand over his face, then cut his eyes to her face. ''I wish you had,'' he said quietly. ''It would make this a hell of a lot easier.''

For some reason she suddenly developed the urge to climb out of the pickup and away from him. But like a foolish puppet, she remained where she was and waited for him to pull the next string.

''''This'? What are you talking about?''

''Me and you. Getting married. Becoming man and wife.''

She straightened her shoulders and turned her face toward the open window. ''Last night in the garden, after we...uh, kissed, I decided getting married would be the wrong thing to do.''

Without warning, his hand was on her bare arm, then his fingers tangled in her loose hair. She forced herself to turn her head toward him, and as her eyes met the odd gleam in his, her breath lodged in her throat.

''Hmm. That's funny. Because last night convinced me getting married is the *only* thing we can do.''

Chapter Five

Long moments passed before Nicole finally talked her lungs into working again, and even then she felt faint.

"Logan...what...are you saying? That you want to marry me for real?"

The question seemed to snap something in him. He dropped his hand from her hair and eased back onto his side of the seat.

"What do you mean by real?"

She made a frustrated gesture with her hand. "Like a true man and wife...sharing a bed together."

Just hearing her say the words fired Logan's loins, and he wondered if coming home had done something to him. Most of his students were older than Nicole. And she was a virgin! She knew nothing about going to bed with a man. For the life of him, he couldn't understand why he found her so damned desirable.

His voice was rough with frustration when he answered, "Uh, no. That's not what I meant."

Her lips parted as she looked at him with confusion. "But you just said—"

He groaned. "Damn it, I know what I just said! But what I meant was...if something like that happened...well, at least we'd be married."

For some ridiculous reason, pain welled up in her chest. She dropped her head and stared at her hands, which were clenched tightly together on her lap.

"You make me sound like I'm some sort of contagious disease you need to stay away from," she said quietly. "And that marriage is an inoculation just in case you do get too close."

Logan hadn't expected this sort of reaction from her. For the past few weeks, since he'd returned to Belle Rouge, she'd been so hard and cynical with him, always ready to toss an insult his way. Now she actually seemed hurt because he didn't want her in his bed!

"Look, Nicole, I admit there's...that something happens when we get near each other. And we both know it doesn't feel all that bad. But I'm not going to marry you to make you my bed partner. That would be an insult to us both."

Would it? she wondered. Nothing about being in his arms felt insulting. It was when she was out of them that she felt she wasn't truly wanted or needed by this man.

"I see. Marrying me for sex is a no-no. But marrying to gain complete control of Belle Rouge is perfectly moral."

His expression hardened. "You take pleasure in making me out the monster, don't you?"

Her head jerked up and her brown eyes snared his gray ones. "I don't understand you, Logan! And furthermore, I think you're lying. You do want to take me

to bed. You just don't want to admit it. Or let yourself
do it. Because I'm a Carrington, and if you did, you'd
be just like your father.''

Was that the true reason? Logan asked himself. No.
Even though it should have, that thought had never
entered his mind. The real reason he couldn't allow
himself to make love to Nicole was far more complex.

"That's not even close to the truth," he said tightly.

"Then what is?" she demanded.

He looked at her for long tense seconds, and then,
with a muttered oath, he reached for her. Dragging her
across the seat, he pulled her into his arms and lowered
his face to within an inch of hers. "Hell yes," he
growled. "I want to make love to you, Nicole! Right
here. Right now. In this heat. With the locusts singing
over our heads.''

Dazed by the sudden switch in him, she reached up
and touched his cheek. "Then why don't you?" she
whispered boldly.

For a few seconds the urge to grind his lips down
on hers was almost more than he could bear. But he
finally managed to lift his head and look away from
her tempting face. "Because I don't want any woman
attached to me in any way.''

Any woman. Maybe her being a Carrington had nothing to do with any of this, after all. The new thought
disturbed her. She could understand why he didn't want
to be connected to her in a serious way. But why other
women?

"And being your wife wouldn't make me an attach-
ment?''

"Not if it was just a legal condition.''

Placing her palms against his chest, she pushed herself away from him. Yet he wouldn't release his hold

on her entirely. His hands splayed against her back, and their warmth radiated through her like a bright shaft of sunlight.

"I think I see now," she said slowly. "You don't want to love anybody."

He swallowed as an odd sort of pain lanced through him. "That's right. I don't."

In all the years Nicole had known Logan, and throughout these past days he'd been back on Belle Rouge, she'd believed she'd known just who and what he was. A hard man. A man who didn't care how much pain he inflicted on others. Because he was incapable of feeling. But now there was something in his face and in his voice that told her otherwise. And she was shocked by the revelation.

"Why, Logan," she said as lightly as she could, "I'm surprised. You of all people ought to be able to keep love and sex separated."

Up until now, he always had kept the two separated, he thought. But there was something about Nicole that messed with his head. When he touched her, he did it with everything inside him. And that scared the hell right out of him. But he had no intentions of letting her know how vulnerable she made him. He wasn't about to give her, or any woman, that much power over him.

"I can keep the two separated. It's you I'm worried about."

She stared at him as she struggled not to feel mortally humiliated. "Me? You think—you have the idea that if we had sex, I'd think it was because you loved me? Dear heavens, Logan, you really are conceited, aren't you?"

His hands moved ever so slightly against her back as his gaze roamed her flushed face. "No. And I'm not

stupid, either. You're still a virgin because you want
to give yourself to a man you love. And I...don't want
that man to be me.''

The bluntness of his words hit her like a hurled rock.
Yet she was determined not to let him see her pain.
She lifted her chin and steadied her voice.

''Believe me, Logan, there's no need for you to
worry. I'd never confuse your lust for love. The emotion just isn't in you.''

His hands dropped from her back as his gray eyes
changed to hard flint. ''That's good. That makes it easy
for both of us. We can be married and take care of all
these legal glitches and not have to be concerned about
any emotional ties getting in the way.''

The man was determined to have everything cold
and businesslike between them, and Nicole suddenly
decided she would give him exactly what he wanted.

It was clear she had to continue to live here for six
months. And if she was going to have any sort of
money to set herself up in a new place, she needed to
sell her shares to him. Marrying him would simplify
everything.

''You're right, Logan. I don't know why I hesitated
about accepting your proposal. It's not like it will mean
anything. You've made me realize signing the marriage
license won't be any more to me than putting my sig-
nature on a cash receipt.''

Her comparison irked him, but there was nothing he
could say. He'd set the ground rules for their marriage;
now he would have to live with them.

''So you are going to marry me?''

Her heart throbbed like an open wound as she gazed
out the window and tried to block the image of his face
from her mind. ''Why not? We need to get this over

and done with. You desperately want Belle Rouge and I…"

"What?" he prompted.

She glanced at him over her shoulder. "I don't want to be beholden to anybody…for anything."

The hardness of her eyes and the rigid straightness of her body said she either hated him or something close to it. Well, that was the way it had to be, he told himself. Cold, distant and safe.

After six months time, Belle Rouge would legally be his and Nicole would move away. But was that going to make him happy? Hell yes, he told himself fiercely. For ten long years, the Carrington women had kept him from his home, and for longer than that the two of them had come between him and his father. In spite of his McNally blood, Logan had been forced to accept that Lyle cared more for his wife and stepdaughter than he had his own son. Of course getting the plantation back and seeing the last of Nicole was going to make him happy. Damn right!

With her back still to him, he said, "We'll drive into Natchitoches this afternoon and get the license. We should be able to be married by the end of the week. Do you want the ceremony to be here in the old house or at the judge's chambers?"

She'd always dreamed of being wed in the church she'd attended since childhood, but she wasn't going to make the suggestion. For her and Logan to be married in a church would be sacrilegious, a mockery of everything she believed in. "Since this is a…legal union, the courthouse ought to do perfectly."

"I'll make the arrangements today."

Nicole didn't realize she'd been holding her breath until the stale air whooshed out of her. "If you've said all you have to say, I need to get back to the house. I have several things to do," she said coolly.

Logan supposed there wasn't anything left to add. She'd consented to marry him. He'd gotten what he wanted. Yet nothing about it felt right or good. Not the way he'd expected it would.

"There's only one thing more," he said quietly.

Her heart stilled. "What is it?"

"Thank you, Nicole. For agreeing to marry me."

Tears suddenly burned in her throat. This wasn't the way it was supposed to be. She should be marrying a man she loved, a man who loved her. Her mother had always dreamed of seeing her daughter walk down the aisle dressed in white lace, with lots of flowers and candles and beautiful music. It was something Simone had missed in her life and she'd wanted the experience for Nicole.

When Nicole had met Bryce and begun to date him seriously, her mother had happily started making wedding plans in the background. When Nicole had discovered he was counterfeit, Simone had been devastated. And Nicole knew her mother would be just as crushed over this loveless match she was about to enter into. She could only be grateful that Simone wasn't alive to see it.

"Don't thank me, Logan. We're both getting what we want."

"Gettin' married today? You and Mr. Logan? Child, have you lost your mind?"

Nicole glanced over her shoulder at Darcy, who was standing in the middle of the bedroom, her hands planted on her ample hips.

Nicole picked up a hairbrush and began to pull it

through her long, tawny mane. "No, I haven't lost my mind. In fact, I think I've finally found it," she told the other woman. "I've come to accept that all men are selfish creatures, Darcy. They're not to be trusted…or loved."

Her face a picture of confusion, the housekeeper walked closer to where Nicole sat at the dressing table. "Then why are you marrying one? I thought you despised Logan."

Nicole inwardly winced at the cruel word Darcy had used. She'd never really despised Logan. Certainly she'd resented him for trying to buy her mother off. But the more she thought about it, the more she realized the insult to Simone wasn't the thing that had caused her feelings toward Logan to fester for all these years.

When she'd first met him, he'd just graduated from LSU with a master's degree in agricultural economics. To Nicole, he'd been unbelievably handsome, ambitious and worldly. For a nearly thirteen-year-old girl who'd never had a sibling, he'd been like a prince, a hero who was going to be her stepbrother. He would love her, protect her, slay dragons for her. Or so she'd foolishly believed. Instead, he couldn't get away from her fast enough. He didn't want anything to do with the illegitimate child of his father's mistress.

"I never hated Logan, Darcy."

"But you don't love the man, either!"

Nicole sighed as she coiled her heavy hair into a chignon at the back of her neck. "No. This marriage has nothing to do with love."

Darcy made a *tsking* noise of disapproval. "Lord help us, I'm glad your mama can't see this. She wouldn't like it. No sir. Not one bit."

Nicole secured her hair with several pins, then, leaving the dressing bench, walked over to the bed, where she'd laid out a dress and undergarments.

The dress was a plain sheath made of pale pink linen. The simple lines made it dressy but not overly so. But how she looked really didn't matter, she told herself. Logan didn't want or expect a beautiful bride. All he wanted was a full deed to Belle Rouge.

"Mother is gone now. And I have to do what I think is best."

Darcy's bushy head swung back and forth. "Sounds to me like you're not thinkin' at all. I thought you wanted a husband who loved you, one you could have kids with. And what about the job you was plannin' on gettin'? You've put that dream aside for a long time now. What's this marriage gonna do to that?"

"You're asking too many questions, Darcy." She sat down on the side of the bed and pulled a pair of sheer panty hose over her toes. "I still want all those things you just said. And I'm going to get them, too. I've just got to postpone my dreams and plans for a while."

Darcy's face wrinkled into lines of disbelief. "For a while! Missy, marriage is supposed to last a lifetime, or haven't you heard that?"

Nicole's lips twisted sardonically. "Not this one. After six months it will all be over. So quit worrying, Darcy. I'm not throwing my life away."

"If you're not throwin' your life away, just exactly what are you doin'?"

Nicole stood and pulled the panty hose up over her hips. "Consolidating my assets."

Darcy groaned, then dropped her face in her hands. Shaking her head with dismay, Nicole went over to the older woman. "Oh, Darcy, please don't be upset like this. Everything will be all right. I promise. This is just a business venture between me and Logan.''

Darcy lifted her head and looked at Nicole with tears in her faded blue eyes. ''Marriage isn't supposed to be about money or business,'' she scolded.

Nicole couldn't hold her gaze. It was simply too painful to see the disapproval in the other woman's eyes. ''Sometimes a woman just doesn't have any other choice, Darcy.''

The housekeeper sniffed. ''Maybe so. But I'll tell you somethin' else, Nicole. Logan is a possessive man. He's not gonna give up anything he owns. And once you become his wife, that'll include you.''

The emphatic words sent a chill of premonition crawling over Nicole's skin. What if Logan began to think of her as one of his possessions? What if he refused to give her a divorce once the six months were up? He could put her through hell if he was so inclined to.

But no, she tried to reassure herself. Logan didn't want her. He'd made that very clear four days ago when they'd driven to the cane fields and she'd agreed to marry him. No, all he wanted was Belle Rouge. And making her his wife was the only way he could get it.

An hour later, Logan and Nicole were traveling the highway that followed the winding Cane River to Natchitoches. She'd not expected to be nervous about the coming ceremony, but the farther north they drove from Belle Rouge, the faster her heart beat.

She told herself her rapid pulse had nothing to do with Logan's appearance. The man was good to look at no matter what he was wearing. But this afternoon in his dark trousers and white shirt, he was the epitome of the powerful McNallys, who had once ruled as cotton kings in the Natchitoches area during the Civil War.

Logan had descended from a long line of strong Irishmen, each of whom in his own way had left his stamp on Belle Rouge. Logan was the last. And would be the last, unless he sired a son.

It was the first time the thought had ever really struck her and she wondered why she'd had to think of such a thing on their wedding day. Not that any of it mattered to her. Someday before he grew old, Logan would probably marry a woman of his own choosing and they'd have a son or daughter, or perhaps several children.

He'd implied he never wanted to love a woman. But Nicole was certain that wouldn't stop him from taking a real wife and having children. He wouldn't be doing it for love. He'd be doing it for Belle Rouge.

"Is your friend Amelia still going to meet us at the courthouse?" Logan asked, breaking the silence in the car.

Nicole glanced across the seat at him and her heart once again lurched into overdrive. "Yes. I told her two-thirty. And she's never late."

"What did she say when you told her we were getting married?"

"Congratulations."

With a mocking quirk of his lips, he glanced at her once more. "Did you explain the situation to her?"

Nicole shrugged. "I told her it was a business merger."

"And?"

Nicole grimaced. "She said, 'Honey, the way you look, the man wants to merge more than business.'"

To her surprise, Logan's head tilted back and deep laughter rolled past his lips. "Sounds like this Amelia knows men."

"She does. But I told her this was one time she was definitely wrong."

The cool stiffness in her voice quickly sobered his laughter. With his gaze fixed on the highway, he said, "Well, she was right about one thing. You are a beautiful woman, Nicole. And whatever you might be thinking, I won't be ashamed to call you my wife."

The gentleness in his voice surprised her far more than his words, and suddenly she desperately wished things could truly be that way between her and Logan. Soft, gentle, loving. It didn't make sense. Yet she wanted that from him. Needed it, in fact.

If he could read her thoughts he would surely be amused, probably even annoyed. But he would never know, she promised herself. One day she would be truly out of his life and she could find someone else, someone who would really love her. And then she could rid herself of this odd fixation she had for Logan McNally.

"Thank you, Logan. And for what it's worth, while we're man and wife, I'll try not to embarrass you. If you want to have affairs, I suppose that's your business, but as for me, I intend to behave as a married woman."

Her avowal took him by complete surprise and he glanced at her again, his eyes drinking in the sober beauty of her face. "Are you doing this for me or the sake of appearances?"

She swallowed and glanced away from him. "My mother spent most of her life trying to shed a reputation. I've learned from her struggles."

As Logan focused his attention back on the highway, he decided Simone Carrington McNally had taught him something, too. Nothing was as it first appeared on the surface. He'd believed the woman was a gold digger, but he was beginning to change his mind about that. From what Thorndyke and his associates had told him, Simone had refused to accept anything of importance from the Belle Rouge estate before her life ended. And now, as he was about to become Nicole's husband, he could only wonder if he was looking at this marriage with a marred vision. Was he crazy to think he could keep it impersonal? He had to. Because there wasn't any way Nicole could ever love him. And hell, he didn't want her to.

As they walked across the parking lot toward the old courthouse, the temperature had to be at the hundred degree mark, Nicole decided. Yet she didn't really notice the heat. Everything around her was taking on a surreal quality and all she could think was that she was about to become Mrs. Logan McNally.

Before they'd left the car, Logan had given her a single white camellia. The flower had taken her by complete surprise and her hands had shaken ever so slightly when she'd pinned it to her dress.

During the ceremony, the pounding of her heart caused the blossom to quiver as though it had a life of its own. And in the back of Nicole's mind she kept wondering why he'd made the romantic gesture. But before she could think of a logical reason, he was slipping a heavy gold band on her finger and the judge was urging him to kiss the bride.

She glanced up at Logan just as he was reaching for her. Then his hand was tilting up her face and his lips met hers. The kiss seemed to go on and on. From some part of the room she heard someone clearing his throat. When Logan eventually released her, she could feel her cheeks were pink, and from the corner of her eye, she could see a look of wry speculation on Amelia's face.

Afterward, as they all signed the marriage document, Amelia said, "I took the liberty of making cake and punch, if you'd like to come by the house."

Nicole glanced at Logan. The idea of them being treated as a couple had never entered her head until now. And as for celebrating the occasion, she didn't necessarily know if it was supposed to be a day of joy.

"It's up to you," she said to him.

Logan glanced from her to Amelia, then smiled as if he'd known the other woman for years rather than a few minutes. "Of course we'll come. It's our wedding day."

If the other woman was surprised that Logan wasn't acting like the cad Nicole had described, she didn't show it. Instead, she smiled at both of them. "Great. I'll see you at my house in a few minutes."

Once Nicole and Logan were in the car, driving away from the courthouse, she said, "You really didn't have to accept Amelia's invitation on my account. We could have gone home."

He shrugged. "We could have. But it was nice of her to go to the trouble to give us a little reception."

She glanced down at her hands, then touched the gold band with the tip of her forefinger. There was something about the stark simplicity of a wedding band, she thought. The piece of jewelry wasn't showy or glittery. It didn't signify money. It represented possession in the most basic, primal way.

"Why did you get a wedding ring for me?"

He didn't answer for long moments, and Nicole was about to decide he was going to ignore the question entirely.

"You're my wife now. I don't want anyone to be mistaken about that."

Suddenly Darcy's words filtered back to her and Nicole nearly shivered on the seat. *Logan is a possessive man. He's not going to give up something he owns.*

Pushing the unsettling thought to the back of her mind, she commented, "I realize this is just a temporary thing, but I thought you might have someone stand up with you."

"My close friends are all back in Shreveport. And this all happened so quickly none of them could manage to get away from their jobs without more notice."

She took her eyes off the ring to look at him. "You never mention your friends or the job you had up there. What are you going to do about your teaching position?"

"I've turned in my resignation," he said flatly.

Nicole's gaze probed his face. "That's a lot to give up."

"Some people will think so. But I acquired a degree in agriculture so I could come back to Belle Rouge and use my knowledge to make the plantation better. I gave up a lot when I went to Shreveport and became a teacher instead."

Yes, Nicole knew exactly what he'd given up. His home. His job. His very life. When she'd come to realize this, she wasn't exactly sure. But little by little since he'd returned she could see that he'd once loved the place. And he still did. That's why, when it came to the bottom line, she could never have left and caused him to lose his home a second time.

"But do you think you'll be happy here now? You've lived in Shreveport for many years. Surely you had lots of friends there you hated to leave. Or a special woman."

His lips twisted and then a faint smile touched his face. "What are all these questions about? Am I seeing a wife's curiosity now?"

A pink flush touched her cheeks. "Maybe. Since you've been back at Belle Rouge, we've never just sat down and talked about regular things. Now that we've settled the problems of your father's will, I was hoping we could be more civil to each other."

His gaze left the traffic for a moment and he glanced at her. "You mean you actually want to declare peace between us?"

The disbelief on his face made her smile, and then, because it felt good to finally be smiling again, she extended her hand across the seat to him.

"I think I'd like that very much," she told him.

He picked up her hand, squeezed it, then rubbed his thumb over the gold band on her finger. "So would I."

The warmth of his hand and the gentleness in his face worked to ease the weight in her heart. Perhaps the next six months weren't going to be filled with the misery she'd first feared. Maybe they could both finally put the past behind them and step into the future as friends and partners.

A smile curved her lips as another idea struck her. "I wonder what your father would say if he could see us now."

Logan chuckled under his breath. "He'd never believe we're married."

Nicole joined in with a giggle of her own. "I'm

certain of that. I think when Lyle wrote that ridiculous will he did it with the idea of punishing us both for not being able to get along.''

"I believe you're right," Logan said. "But we got the last laugh on the old man. In six months time, Lyle McNally's will won't mean a damn thing. I'll have what I want and you'll have what you want. Isn't that the way you see it?''

Nicole supposed so. He'd have Belle Rouge. She'd have money and the freedom to pursue a career as an accountant, perhaps even build an accounting firm of her own. So why was she suddenly feeling so hollow inside? she wondered.

"Exactly," she forced herself to agree, then motioned toward the next intersection. "Turn here. You have to cross the river to get to Amelia's."

Once Logan pulled to a stop in the short driveway, he killed the motor, then turned toward Nicole. "Before we go in, I thought I'd answer your question," he said.

Her brows arched upward. "What question?"

"The one about the special woman back in Shreveport."

Everything inside her went still. "And?"

His eyes looked into hers. "There isn't one."

She swallowed as the urge to lean into him, to place her lips on his gripped her like an iron fist. "You didn't have to tell me this. It really doesn't matter," she said huskily.

"I guess not. But you're my wife now. And I thought you had a right to know."

She didn't know what to say. What could she say when all she really wanted to do was kiss him, feel his arms around her? *Oh God, don't let it start,* she prayed. *Don't let this man break my heart.*

"I think we'd better go in," she said softly.

"In a minute," he assured her, then leaning closer, he brushed his fingertips against her cheek. "You look very beautiful today, Nicole. A radiant virgin bride."

The touch of his hand and the raw look of wanting on his face was suddenly more than she could resist. With a little cry of anguish, she whispered, "Logan, don't!"

Her plea went unheard. Groaning, he jerked her into his arms and covered her mouth with his.

Nicole flung her arms around his neck and buried herself against him. As he thrust his tongue past her hungry lips, it dawned on her that this was what she really needed from Logan. Not money. Not Belle Rouge. Just him. And his love.

Chapter Six

Logan jabbed his pocketknife deep into the loose soil at the base of the plant and began to dig toward the root system.

"I didn't notice anything was wrong until a few of the plants started listing," the farm manager said. "I wish like hell I'd noticed it sooner."

"Don't feel badly, Leo. I've been all over these fields and I didn't pick up on a problem." He glanced up at the older man, who'd been the manager at Belle Rouge for many long years. Even though Logan had far more formal education, he respected and admired Leo's firsthand experience. "Do you think this is the only spot that's affected?"

"Me and several of the men have made random digs in all the other fields. This is the only trouble spot we could find."

"That's encouraging. Maybe we can figure out what this little monster is before it decides to spread."

Logan whacked off a part of the diseased root, then

straightened to his full height. Thankfully, the sun was blazing this afternoon, but for the past two weeks rain had fallen nearly every day. If they didn't have a few days of dry weather, everything was going to mildew.

"You think the problem is the soggy ground?"

"Well, this is probably the lowest spot on the property." He handed the web of roots to Leo. "But we won't know until we get this tested. Run it up to the university at Shreveport and see what they can come up with in their lab. If it turns out we can treat the problem with a chemical, get it while you're there. If not, we might have to destroy this part of the field."

Not wasting any time, Leo nodded and headed toward a white pickup truck with Belle Rouge Plantation emblazoned in red on the side of the door. "I'll let you know as soon as I find out anything."

Logan waved him off and was about to head to his own truck when he heard a noise from behind him. Glancing around, he saw Nicole riding up on Dumpling. The gray horse was sweating, and from the looks of Nicole's flushed face, so was she.

"What are you doing out here?" he asked as she pulled the horse to a stop and swung her leg over the saddle.

"After all the rain, I'm enjoying the sun," she said with a smile.

Not nearly as much as he was enjoying looking at his new wife. Her thick, red-gold hair was tied casually at the base of her neck with a wide blue ribbon. Faded jeans clung to her long shapely legs and the V neck of her white blouse exposed a triangle of creamy, smooth skin. But it was the smile on her face that warmed him the most.

So far in the two weeks since they'd married, peace

had remained between them. And except for the passionate kiss they'd shared in front of Amelia's house, Logan had managed to keep his hands to himself. Barely.

Walking over to her left stirrup, he held up his arms. "Coming down?"

She nodded. "I need to stretch my legs."

She reached to grip his shoulders, and his hands lightly circled her waist as he eased her down to the ground beside him.

The scent of flowers drifted from her hair and skin to tease his senses. One tug of his hands was all it would take to have her in his arms, but the consequences that might produce forced him to release his hold on her waist and step back.

"You've made Dumpling hot," he remarked, glancing beyond her shoulder to the horse's sweaty neck.

"I didn't do that to him. He did it to himself. *He* wanted to run. I was perfectly content to walk."

"Can't you control him?"

She laughed and the sound rippled through him like rich wine. Not since his ordeal with Tracie had he allowed himself to notice the little things about a woman. Her laugh, her sighs. The scent of her skin, the subtle shades in her eyes. He'd forgotten how intoxicating all those things could be. Or maybe he'd never really known, until he'd come back to Belle Rouge and made Nicole his wife.

"Of course. Dumpling will do anything I ask him to. So I decided to let him have his way for a while."

"In other words, you've been spoiling him."

Her smile deepened as she turned and stroked the gelding's nose. "He's worth it, aren't you, sweet boy?"

Logan let out a long breath as he imagined what it might be like if she stroked him with such affection.

"I suppose you'll want to take Dumpling with you when you leave Belle Rouge," he said.

She didn't look at him. "No. He belongs on the plantation. It's always been his home."

"But you obviously love the horse," Logan reasoned.

"It's because I love him that I want him to stay here."

"I'm not sure I understand."

She turned a wan smile on him. "I want him to be happy. Uprooting him from his home would be cruel. The same goes for Sally. She'd be miserable if she couldn't hunt for squirrels and coons or sleep on the porch or get the leftovers of Darcy's red-eye gravy."

Nicole was right. Yet Logan didn't want to think about her giving up the pets she so loved or her home here at Belle Rouge. But he quickly reminded himself she would be amply compensated. Giving up her share of the plantation would give her plenty of capital to do whatever she wanted, go wherever her heart desired. And in return he'd be on his own. Alone. With no one to worry about but himself. It would be worth it, he promised himself.

"I've sent Leo to Shreveport to get a test on the rotted roots," he told her.

Concern marred her forehead as she glanced at him. "Neither one of you could tell what it is?"

"I've seen a lot of plant diseases over the years, but nothing exactly like this."

She looked out at the field of cane. In the past weeks since Logan had come home, he'd worked incessantly with the field hands. At first she'd thought his only

intentions were to flaunt his authority and make sure
all the men knew he was now the boss in charge. But
slowly over the past weeks it had become evident to
Nicole that he was working alongside with them, rather
than over them. He respected his employees. And she
admired him greatly for that and for the tireless devotion he gave to Belle Rouge.

Turning to face him, she asked, "Is there a danger
of losing much of the crop?"

"I don't intend to let the problem get out of hand.
Hopefully we can find something to check the spread
of this thing, whatever it turns out to be."

No, he wouldn't let the problem get out of hand, she
thought. He'd do his best to get control of the situation.
The same way he'd restrained himself and turned his
self-control to iron since their marriage. Which was a
bit of a surprise to Nicole. The kiss they'd shared in
Amelia's driveway the day of their wedding had been
anything but restrained.

Thinking back on it, Nicole wasn't sure they would
have ever made it into the house if it hadn't been for
the stifling heat inside the car and the loud barking of
the next-door neighbor's nosy dog.

"I understand how important it is to you to produce
a good crop. And not just for the profit," she said.

He appeared surprised and pleased by her comment.
"Maybe you do know me. A little," he added with a
grin.

"I'm learning," she said. And the more she learned,
the more she grew to respect this complex man she'd
married. "Well, I'm sure you have things to do," she
continued, "but before I head back to the house, I
wanted to let you know Thorndyke has the papers
ready for us to sign. I told him to have someone drop

them by later this afternoon and we'd be available to sign them.''

''I'll be there,'' he assured her.

As she reached for Dumpling's reins, she felt Logan's presence behind her, then his hands were on the back of her waist. Today was the first time he'd had reason to touch her in days, and as the warmth of his fingers spread through her, she realized how much she'd missed being in his arms, feeling his lips on hers.

''Nicole?''

''Yes.''

''You do want to do this, don't you? I'm not going to force you to give up your share of Belle Rouge.''

He *was* forcing her, in a way. But Nicole had to admit it wasn't entirely his fault. If they could've somehow been like regular stepbrother and sister they might have been able to both continue living here together indefinitely. As it was, the sexual tension between them was too explosive to chance anything more than six months.

''I understand that. It's…this is just the way it has to be, Logan,'' she said quietly. Then before he could say more, she lifted her leg and jammed the toe of her boot in the stirrup. ''Help me up, would you?''

He lifted her easily into the saddle, and after she'd settled herself in the seat, she started to rein Dumpling back toward the house. But Logan caught the toe of her boot with his hand forcing her to wait.

She looked anxiously down at him. ''Is something wrong?''

Only everything, he thought. He didn't wish to take this place, and everything she held dear, away from her. He didn't want to hurt her. And most of all he didn't want to feel this incessant desire he had for her.

What was the matter with him? Why couldn't he forget about Nicole and concentrate on the real reason he'd come back—for Belle Rouge and Belle Rouge only?

"It's nothing. I'll be back at the house shortly."

An associate of Thorndyke's arrived at four o'clock that evening. Darcy ushered the young man into the parlor, and Nicole invited him back to the study, where Logan was working at his desk.

"Would you like a drink, Mr. Denton?" Nicole asked as the lawyer took a seat on a long, leather couch.

"A Scotch and water would be nice, Miss Carrington."

Logan gave him a hard glare. "Her name is Mrs. McNally."

The young man looked properly chastised. "Well, uh, yes, it is her legal name."

"It's her *only* name," he said tightly, then called out to Nicole, who was crossing the room to a small table loaded with all sorts of spirits. "Leave it. Darcy will fix the man a drink."

She looked at him with raised brows, then returned to where the two men were and took a seat in an armchair.

Logan picked up the telephone on his desk and jabbed one number. "Darcy, we need you in the study," he said, then tossed the receiver back on its hook.

The young lawyer reached nervously for his briefcase. "Well, I think you'll find the terms of the agreement all in order. Of course, both of you should look them over before you sign." He glanced at Logan, who'd left his seat and had moved around to the front of the desk. "We, uh, want you and Miss—I mean Mrs. McNally—to be happy, uh, once you divorce."

Divorce. To Logan, the word was like bitter gall. And from the look of open appreciation on the young lawyer's face when his eyes were on Nicole, he couldn't wait for the whole thing to happen, Logan decided.

"You read them first, Logan," Nicole urged him. "My forte is numbers. You might have to explain some of the legal jargon to me."

"That's what I'm here for," the lawyer quickly told her.

Thankfully, Darcy chose that minute to step into the study. Otherwise, Logan was certain he would have jerked the man to his feet and booted his behind out the door.

"I'd rather have my husband explain things to me," Nicole said, surprising both men.

Denton handed the papers to Logan. While he read, the lawyer sipped the drink Nicole had instructed Darcy to make for him.

From the corner of her eye, she could watch Logan, and as each minute passed his face grew harder. She wasn't sure if his reaction was due to the contents of the legal document or the covert glances the young lawyer was tossing her way every few moments. It would be crazy to think Logan might be jealous of her. But then she couldn't forget that evening she'd come home from visiting Thorndyke's office. Logan had admitted he didn't want to think of any man's hands on her.

Just as she wouldn't want that sort of attention from anyone but Logan, Nicole thought dourly. Denton was a nice-enough-looking man. His suit and tie appeared expensive and professional, his dark blond hair was combed perfectly, his wide smile was full of straight white teeth. But he was much too soft and full of himself to be her type.

Her gaze slipped back to Logan. His workboots were planted slightly apart and caked with delta mud. Worn jeans clung to his hard-muscled thighs. A navy-blue T-shirt stretched across his broad chest and exposed his strong arms. He was a highly intelligent, educated man. Yet he was also a simple man of the land. The mixture greatly appealed to Nicole. Yet deep down she knew it wasn't just the way Logan looked, what he knew or the job he did that made her want him. It was something undefinable. Something that made her heart ache just a little whenever she saw him smile.

"Well, everything looks in order to me." He walked over to Nicole's chair and handed her the agreement. "Read it carefully. I want to make sure you understand everything it says."

She took the papers from him and slowly read the contents. After all the legal jargon was stripped away, it basically said she was signing over her spouse's share of Belle Rouge to Logan and also her own share. But neither transfer would become legal until six months had been lived out together. Once the shares became Logan's, he would pay her a fair and marketable price, to be agreed upon once their marriage was dissolved.

It was a business deal. Plain and simple. There wasn't anything written about wanting or needing or loving and hurting. But then, she wasn't supposed to feel any of those things during this marriage. And neither was Logan.

"It looks clear and concise to me." She stood and

handed the document back to Logan. "I'm ready to sign, if you are."

Logan glanced at Thorndyke's associate. "What if one of us changes our mind before the six months are up?"

"It wouldn't do you any good. Once you both sign the contract, you're both committed."

Logan turned a questioning look on Nicole. "Does that idea bother you?"

From the couch, Denton spoke up. "If you'd like, we can write an appendage stating that either one of you may have the opportunity to change your mind at the end of the six months. Of course, both of you would have to sign it. And I'm sure you understand it would weaken the contract as a whole."

"I don't need a safety valve," Nicole quickly announced. Selling out to Logan was the only choice she had. To try to continue living here with him under any circumstances would be crazy. She didn't want to spend the next six months in indecision about her future. She wanted the break between them to be clean and swift, not lingering and painful. "I'm ready to sign the agreement as it is."

"Fine. You've made a wise decision, Mrs. McNally." Smiling at her, Denton rose to his feet and pulled a pen from inside his suit jacket. "I'll show you where to sign."

"Not so fast!" Logan interjected. "I haven't said I'm agreeable yet."

Nicole practically gasped. "But, Logan, this contract is what *you* wanted! Why would you ask the lawyers to write an appendage? We both know this is the way things have to be!"

Was it? Logan asked himself. Did he really believe

Nicole's leaving and him owning all of Belle Rouge would make him happy? It had to, he silently told himself. He couldn't live with Nicole and not want her. And he sure as hell wasn't going to risk putting his heart in her hands. She might not be deceptive like Tracie, but she was a woman. And as far as Logan was concerned, none of them were dependable or trustworthy. If nothing else, his mother's alcoholism had taught him that much.

Clara had thought being Lyle McNally's wife would be enough to keep her happy. But in reality, the slow, quiet life here at Belle Rouge had eventually made her crazy. Nicole was still very young; she didn't need to be buried on this place. He knew that even if she didn't.

"You're right," he said abruptly. "Let's sign this thing and be done with it."

Not wasting any more time or words, he carried the contract to a nearby table. Denton and Nicole quickly followed, and in less than five minutes the whole thing was over with and the papers left with the lawyer, to be notarized and filed away.

"Well," Nicole said, trying to smile, "I guess we can finally put that out of our minds." She glanced around her, while thinking how quiet and empty the room seemed after something so monumental had just taken place in it. "Maybe we should have a drink ourselves," she suggested.

"What for?" he said tersely.

"To celebrate. I'm sure it gives you a good feeling to know Belle Rouge is finally all yours."

Logan groaned. "Nicole, please let's not argue—"

"Logan, I'm truly sincere about this," she interrupted, amazed that her feelings toward him had softened so much in the past few weeks. But since their marriage, Nicole had done a lot of thinking, and though it had hurt, she'd forced herself to look at things through his eyes. He'd lost his mother in a tragic accident, then his father had quickly married his mistress and moved her into Belle Rouge. If Nicole had been in Logan's shoes, she would have probably felt as though she was being shoved aside, too. It was past time for him to have his home back. "I'm glad the place belongs solely to you now. That's the way it should be."

He studied her through narrowed eyes. "You really mean that, don't you?"

She nodded, then, letting out a long breath, she walked over to a window that overlooked the pecan grove. The lines of huge trees stretched endlessly, their thick leaves making a green roof. Down through the years, she and Sally had used the orchard for their walks, and in the fall, Nicole always picked some of the fallen nuts by hand and helped Darcy make pecan pralines. She supposed those times would soon be over. She would miss Belle Rouge. But she was deeply afraid she was going to miss Logan far more.

"Yes. I do," she said huskily. Then, turning back to him, she smiled. "Your ancestors built this place. It should always belong to a McNally."

She was a McNally, too, now that they were married. But he didn't remind her of the fact. Theirs wasn't that sort of marriage.

Walking over to where she continued to stand by the window, he said, "You're being very generous about this."

A wan smile touched her lips as she looked up at his ruggedly etched face. "I guess that surprises you."

"A great deal. You didn't exactly throw out the welcome mat for me when I returned a few weeks ago."

"No. I felt invaded," she said, while realizing it had really been her heart he'd intruded on and not her home. But that was something she was going to make sure he never knew.

"I'm sorry."

The simple words touched her far more than anything else could have. She didn't expect he said them often, if ever.

"Don't be," she said gently. "I was still grieving over losing Mother. I think for a while a part of me was dead, too. But now...well, I probably said some awful things to you that I don't even remember. If I did, please forget them."

Since they had married and formed a truce of sorts, Logan had begun to wonder if the Nicole he'd first come home to was the real one or if it was this gentler, more understanding young woman before him. No matter, he thought wryly. Both were equally hard to resist.

"They're already forgotten," he replied.

A soft smile lit her face. "Well, I really was serious about the drink. I think we should have some sort of toast or something."

If she was happy about the occasion, he had to be, too, Logan told himself. "We'll have wine tonight with supper," he said as an idea suddenly took place in his head. "Have you ever been to Lafayette?"

One tawny brow arched with curiosity. "Once. Why?"

"I thought we might drive down there tonight and have supper."

She stared at him. "Supper! But it's a hundred miles down there!"

He chuckled. "A little more. But who's counting? There's a place down there that has great seafood and the best Cajun music you've ever heard."

If they weren't already married, the whole thing would sound suspiciously like a date, and the idea made her heart flutter. "When I said we should cele-brate with a toast, I wasn't hinting for a night out."

He shrugged. "I didn't think you were. But I believe you'll agree with me that none of this has been easy for either of us. A night out and away from Belle Rouge will do us both good."

Excitement suddenly poured through her. It had been so long, ages in fact, since she'd been anywhere other than to college or running an errand. As for going out with a man, Bryce had ruined all that. She hadn't let herself trust one long enough to take her to the grocery store, much less an intimate dinner for two. But Logan was different. He was her husband.

"I think you're right," she agreed, her eyes lighting up. "How soon should we leave?"

He glanced at his watch. "We need to be on the road in thirty minutes."

"I'll be ready," she assured him.

The drive to Lafayette took three hours, but Logan didn't notice the time behind the wheel or the gnawing hunger in his stomach. The sight of Nicole in the seat next to him was more than a distraction.

Although her long broomstick skirt and roper boots hid her legs, her silky apricot blouse dipped at the neckline, revealing the smooth white skin just above her breasts. She was like other Southern women who took pains to keep their complexion guarded from the sun. And it showed on Nicole. Every inch that was exposed to his eyes was like a gorgeous piece of satin.

Several times already tonight he'd caught himself wondering if the rest of her body was as soft and smooth and creamy as the parts he could see.

Yet it wasn't just her appearance that had caught Logan's attention. He'd never seen her so animated or absorbed by the sights around her. Seeing the enjoyment on her face made him feel rather guilty that he'd not taken her out before tonight. For some reason he didn't understand, it was especially important to him that she be happy while they were married.

"How long has it been since you've been down this way?" he casually asked.

She turned her head away from the passenger window to look at him. "Maybe three years. I'm not sure. Why?"

"No particular reason. I was just wondering if you got out much after your mother had the stroke."

The faint smile on her face disappeared. "No. I didn't like to leave her with a health provider unless it was necessary."

"Your mother was handicapped for more than two years. That's a long time to be tied down."

"I wasn't tied down—I finished college," she reasoned.

But she couldn't have dated much, he decided. Otherwise, she wouldn't still be a virgin.

"The day of our wedding, I overheard your friend Amelia mentioning something about you finding a job as an accountant. Is that what you want to do?"

"I've always liked working with numbers. And I never planned to just sit at Belle Rouge and twiddle my thumbs. But when Mother had the stroke, just getting through college was tough enough. I had to postpone my plans to find a permanent job as an accountant. I thought about doing some freelancing on my own, but with her health being so unstable, I decided I shouldn't commit to something I might not be able to handle. So I...put things off.''

He could hear disappointment in her voice. Obviously starting a career was important to her. And that surprised Logan. All these years, he'd figured Nicole would be content to let Belle Rouge support her. But with each day he was learning she was not the woman he'd first imagined her to be. She was strong and proud.

''You haven't been out looking for a job now, have you?''

Surprised, she glanced at him again. ''No. Not yet. I—don't want to start a new job with a company and then have to quit and move. I guess I'll just wait until the six months at Belle Rouge are up before I make any permanent decisions about where I want to go.'' She grimaced. ''Besides, I don't have any job experience yet, so I might have to move to a much larger city to get hired.''

So she wasn't making any firm plans about her future until their marriage was over. For some reason the news relieved Logan. He didn't want to think about her moving to a big city, where she would be exposed to all sorts of dangers. And he would never get to see her.

''You know, Nicole, you really won't have to work, if you don't want to. The money you get for your shares of Belle Rouge will be enough to keep you comfortable. Especially if you invest part of it wisely.''

She frowned at him. ''Not work? Logan, I'm not a shiftless person. I want—no, I *need* to be a productive human being to be happy.''

He shrugged, then surprised himself by saying, "Being a wife and mother would be very productive."

At one time in her life, Nicole had wanted more than anything to be those things. Being raised without a father or siblings had made her crave a true family of her own. But after Bryce had fooled and humiliated her, she'd taken another look at her life. Particularly the men who'd affected it.

Her father had cut out without even bothering to marry her mother. And though she'd loved her stepfather, Lyle had cheated on an alcoholic wife and eventually married his mistress. For ten years Logan had deserted his father and turned his nose up at her and Simone. After swearing he'd love her forever, Bryce had made a quick exit. It was obvious to Nicole that men as a whole weren't dependable for the long haul. The best thing she could do for herself was remember that.

"The job requires a man," she said tersely. "And I don't want one."

Logan's dark brows quirked upward. "Ever?"

She gazed out the window at the growing darkness. "Not if I can help it."

"But you're only twenty-two," he reasoned.

She snorted beneath her breath. "You were twenty-two at one time. I don't see you with a woman."

"I have a wife."

"Not the real kind," she said, then turned a knowing glance on him. "You don't want a real wife or family. You said so."

He certainly had. For years he'd said it over and over to himself. Until he'd finally convinced himself he'd be better off living his life alone. And he was. He damned sure was.

Across from him, Nicole wistfully touched the gold band circling her finger. "But you will have a real wife one day," she continued. "You won't let the McNally name end with you. You'll have to sire a son before you die."

A son. A part of his flesh and—his eyes drifted over to Nicole—a part of hers? *Dear Lord, don't let me even think it,* he prayed.

But as the miles continued to slip past them, he kept picturing Nicole's naked body beneath his, the feel of her arms around him, the taste of her lips. Then the sight of her growing waist and finally a baby suckling at her breast.

Wondering if he was losing his mind, or actually coming to his senses, Logan turned his head and allowed his gaze to settle on her comely face. No one had to remind him that the McNally name and the possession of Belle Rouge Plantation would eventually end with him if he didn't produce an heir. The thought struck him often, especially since he'd passed thirty.

But having a child also included a wife, and ties that couldn't be easily severed. He'd told himself it didn't matter if the McNally name expired along with him. The end of the McNally dynasty wouldn't be nearly as disastrous as a divorce or nasty custody battle where an innocent child would come out the victim. He knew all too well what it was like as a child to have two warring parents.

And yet Nicole was already his wife, and he somehow knew she would be a good mother to his baby. The respect and devotion she'd had for her own mother told him that much.

"Tell me, Nicole, are you offering to bear me a son?"

He was kidding, of course. Nicole knew he was. He would someday want a child. But not now and certainly not with her.

She took a deep breath and let it out before she said, "A child should be conceived and born out of love. I couldn't do it any other way. And we both know that doesn't fit your plans."

No, it didn't fit his plans, and he could never pretend with Nicole just to get himself an heir. He respected her too much for that sort of deceit.

He grimaced. "You're right. When two people have a child they should be in love." He shrugged, then glanced at her. "Oh well, Dad is gone. He'll never know the bloodline ended with me. Besides, there are worse things."

"Like marrying a woman for love, I suppose," she said. Then, to her relief, she suddenly spotted the lights of Lafayette looming ahead of them. "Oh good, it looks like we're about to head into the city. I'm starving. Are you?"

Not until tonight and this very moment did Logan realize what a starved man he really was. Not only for a woman's body, but for love, companionship, a family. All the things a man was put on this earth to acquire and enjoy. But would he ever be brave enough to reach for them? he wondered.

"I'm hungry," he admitted. "But I can wait."

Chapter Seven

"I've never eaten anything so delicious in my life,"
Nicole told him as her fingers nimbly broke open the
crawfish tail. She popped the morsel of meat into her
mouth and relished the unique flavor.

"I can order more if you want them," he teased.

Nicole laughed. Between them, on the small table-
top, a large basketful of boiled crawfish were waiting
to be eaten. But that was just the appetizer. Later would
come the gumbo and jambalaya, the fried catfish and
fantail shrimp.

"You're going to have to help me eat these or I'll
be too full to eat anything else," she declared.

Grinning, he shook his head. "I'm not a crawfish
eater."

"How do you know you're not? Surely you've eaten
them before."

"No."

She stared at him as if he'd just told her he was from
Mars. "Good gracious, Logan, you're a born-and-bred

Louisianian and you haven't eaten a crawfish? Shame on you!''

He laughed. "Well, I just never could bring myself to eat something I played with as a boy."

She cleaned another tail, then, after dipping it into spicy red sauce, held it out to him. "Here. Try one. I dare you."

At any other time and with anyone else, Logan would have refused. But they were in Randall's, where the atmosphere was down-home. The huge open room had a planked floor and wooden beams holding up the ceiling. The chairs around the cloth-covered tables were twine-bottomed, the kind set out on porches, that men tilted against the wall while they whittled. The place was packed with couples both young and old, some with children, some without. A few feet away from them, at one end of the parquet dance floor, a Cajun band was warming up their instruments. It was a place to let your hair down, forget your troubles and simply enjoy being with the person sitting across from you.

"All right," he agreed. "But if I get sick, just remember you'll be the one to drive home."

She laughed at his warning. "The only way you're going to get sick is from eating too many of them."

The spicy crawfish had a distinctive flavor, unlike anything Logan had ever tasted. He had to admit they were delicious. "Okay, so they're good. Now you have to clean me another one."

"Oh, no. You're going to do your own cleaning."

He feigned a wounded look. "But I don't know how."

She gave him a smug smile. "I'm sure you're a fast learner. I'll show you."

After a few bumbled attempts, which brought fits of laughter from Nicole, he got the hang of stripping the hard shell away from the crawfish tail. Soon, both of them had a pile of discarded shells before them, and the bottle of wine he'd ordered to accompany their meal was nearly half-empty.

"How did you know about this place?" she asked, leaning back in her chair. The crawfish had whetted her appetite and the wine had left her warm and relaxed. For the first time in a long time, she felt as if her world was finally going to become a brighter place.

"Oh, during my tenure at LSU I had to travel to quite a few speaking engagements. While I was here in Lafayette a few years ago, I was hunting for a good place to eat and someone told me about Randall's. Whenever I'm down this way and have the chance, I drop in for at least one meal."

She regarded him for long moments. "You don't miss your job."

His lips twisted as he reached for his wineglass. "How do you know that?"

"I just do. I think you were born to work the land. Not be confined in a classroom. Or any room, for that matter."

That she could see inside him so well actually startled Logan. Even though he and Nicole had shared several passionate kisses, they hadn't spent much time together. Most of the time their conversations were brief and essential or mundane and impersonal. He hadn't expected her to know about or understand anything he'd been feeling since he'd come home to Belle Rouge.

"You're right. And I'm sorry I stayed away from the place for so long."

Surprised by his comment, she leaned forward. "Really? That's…very hard for me to believe. You were…so bitter when you first returned."

His eyes touched hers, then dropped to her full, moist lips. "So were you."

She sighed. "I guess we were both hurt by our parents."

He tried not to think about her lips. But each time she smiled, each glance she gave him made him want to lean across the table and taste her.

"You've always fiercely stood by your mother," he pointed out.

"That's true. Because I loved her. But she should've never had an affair with a married man."

Even a few weeks ago, Logan would have gloated over Nicole's concession. To hear her say her mother had been wrong would have been a great victory for him. Now it only saddened him, because he could see how much Nicole had suffered from the choices her mother had made.

He nodded. "And even though he was unhappy with my mother, my father should have never had a roaming eye. Simone and Lyle were both wrong."

"They were both human," Nicole said softly.

So was he, Logan thought. And he wondered how much longer he could keep thinking of Nicole as just a woman wearing his name.

Their main course arrived soon after and they leisurely enjoyed the rich, spicy food. By the time they couldn't eat another bite, the band was playing full force and happy Cajun yells could be heard now and then around the room.

Nicole couldn't remain still as the fast beat vibrated off the walls. Even though she couldn't understand any of the French lyrics, her toes tapped the floor, her shoulders swayed and her eyes glowed as she watched the dancers circle the crowded dance floor.

"If you're finished with your coffee, let's go take a whirl," Logan suggested.

She looked astonished. "You can dance?"

He chuckled. "Among other things."

She quickly jumped to her feet and reached for his hand. "Show me, Mr. McNally."

Logan did more than show Nicole he could dance. He whirled, dipped, two-stepped and waltzed her until she was laughing and out of breath. Each time a song ended, she expected him to guide her back to their table, but that never happened, and soon she realized he had no intention of sitting back down.

To her utter surprise, Logan was in his element on the dance floor and was enjoying every minute of it. She'd never seen him laugh or smile before. At least not with such frequent abandon. And the transformation went straight to her heart. So much so that by the time the band finally played a slow tune and Logan pulled her into his arms, she melted against him. Her hand clung to his, her other arm went round his neck and her cheek pressed against his.

Logan had known it would be a mistake to dance with her this closely. Every pore in his body was reacting to her softness, the sweet scent on her hair and skin and the trusting way she clung to him. Each little movement caused her breasts to press into his chest, her thighs to brush against his.

What little wine he'd consumed had worn off hours ago, but he'd never felt so drunk with wanting. He didn't want this time with her to end. But once the music stopped, the band began to pack up their instruments.

"It looks like it's time to go," he said as she slowly stepped out of his arms.

Dreamy-eyed, she nodded and allowed him to lead her off the dance floor. Outside, the night was hot and muggy, cloaking them like dark velvet.

As Logan helped her into the car, she realized she was much more tired than she'd first thought. She sank gratefully into the leather seat and leaned her head back.

While Logan negotiated the late-night city traffic, she didn't distract him with conversation, but once they were traveling north on the open interstate, she reached over to him with her hand.

He clasped his fingers around hers while casting her a brief smile.

"I really had a wonderful time tonight, Logan. Thank you."

"You're welcome."

"Are you too tired to make the drive home?"

It would be hours before the ache in his body let him sleep. Once they got back to Belle Rouge he was going to stand in a cold shower for thirty minutes and hope that would be enough to wash the feel of her from his mind.

"No. I'll be fine. You go to sleep."

She let out a contented sigh and closed her eyes. "I don't want to sleep. I want to think about the food and the music. And the people. They were all so happy, so carefree."

A strange emotion suddenly tightened his throat. "So were we," he said.

"Yes. So were we," she echoed. Then, before she

could let herself be sad about leaving him and Belle Rouge, she squeezed his hand and drifted off to sleep.

It was the wee hours of the morning before Logan finally pulled the car to a stop in front of the big old house. Nicole was still asleep, her head slumped against his shoulder.

Gently, he eased her back into the seat, then left the car and went around to the passenger door. When he lifted her out of the vehicle and into his arms, she groaned in protest.

"Put your arms around my neck," he gently instructed.

Still half-asleep, she did as he asked, then buried her face in his strong shoulder. It wasn't until they were in the house and halfway up the staircase that she realized they were home and he was carrying her.

"Logan!" she whispered loudly. "I'm awake now. You can put me down before you strain your back."

With a strange glitter in his eyes, he continued on up the stairs. "My back isn't being strained. It still feels like we're dancing."

The memory of the closeness she'd shared with him at Randall's filled her with warmth. She lifted her head from his shoulder and her heart went still as she saw the hungry look on his face. She breathed his name and he bent his head and kissed her.

The next thing she knew they were in his bedroom and he was laying her across a high, four-poster bed. He didn't give her time to think or wonder. His mouth crushed down on hers; his hands tugged at the buttons on her blouse.

Soon he had the silky fabric parted, and his lips left hers to explore the soft mounds of flesh spilling over her lacy bra. Desire flamed through her like a burning arrow, sending a hot ache to the lower region of her body.

Groaning with need, she thrust her hands in his hair and urged his lips back to hers. Eager to comply, he plunged his tongue deep into the warm recesses of her mouth, where he explored the ridges along the roof, the sharp edges of her teeth and finally the outer curve of her lips.

"I know this isn't suppose to be happening," he whispered between raspy breaths. "But I want you, Nicole! Heaven help me, I want you!"

And she wanted him just as badly. It didn't matter what had gone on in the past. It didn't matter what might happen in the future. The only thing she could think about was having his hard, warm body joining hers, loving hers.

Gripping his shoulders, she gasped. "I know, Logan. I know. No one has ever made me feel like this. No one. Ever. Show me the rest. Make me yours."

Her pleas were like gasoline on an already raging fire, and his hands began to shake as he stripped away the rest of her clothing. From a nearby window, moonlight filtered through the branches of a live oak and danced along her porcelain-white skin like dark, eager fingers. And when Logan bent his head and touched his tongue to the valley between her breasts, she tasted like rich sweet cream.

Like a cat, he lapped and savored all the way from her throat to the faint indention of her belly button. Her full, round breasts filled his hands. He raised their luscious weight to his lips, then teased the already rigid nipples with his tongue.

By the time he lifted his head, Nicole was writhing with desperate need. She fumbled with the buttons on his shirt, but her hands were shaking too badly to make any progress.

He eased away from her long enough to shed his clothing, then rejoined her on the bed, gathering her tightly into his arms.

The shock of his bare body next to her caused her to gasp out loud, and for a moment he looked at her with faint regret.

"This is crazy," he whispered urgently. "You don't need this—"

She smothered the rest of his words with a long, urgent kiss. "You're my husband, Logan. My *husband*. And I want you."

He couldn't resist her. He'd been a fool to think he ever could. "Nicki! Oh, Nicki, you're so beautiful. Too beautiful."

Her thick, red-gold hair lay in tangled waves upon her white shoulders. He shoved his hands into the silky strands, then, framing her face with his palms, he brought his lips close to hers. "Don't let me hurt you," he implored, his voice choked with desire.

Her arms tightly circled his neck. "You won't, darling. Don't think about it. Just love me."

She wound her legs around his, and it was the last invitation he needed. Urgently, he rolled her onto her back and parted her thighs. Then, with one slow thrust, he was past the barrier of her innocence and her soft warm body was surrounding him, shocking him with a pleasure too great to bear.

Somewhere among his splintering senses, he could hear her groaning his name. He forced himself to pause, bend his head and kiss away the pain.

"Are you all right?" he whispered.

Dazed, she looked up at him, and then awed rapture slowly spread across her face.

"Yes. Oh, yes! Don't stop. Don't let me go, Logan. Ever."

Her hips lifted to his, underscoring her eager pleas. His body on fire, he began to move inside her. And as he did he felt as though he'd wanted Nicole all of his life. She was the center of everything he had and all that he would ever need.

All too soon, he was gripping her waist, grinding her hips into the mattress and calling her name as his desire spilled hotly inside her.

When awareness began to slowly surface, he realized he'd collapsed on Nicole and she was struggling to catch her breath.

Quickly he rolled away from her, but kept one hand possessively on her breast. "Are you all right?"

Her lips tilted upward in an expression of exhausted bliss. "That's the second time you've asked me. I'm beginning to think you're afraid you're going to break me like a china doll."

Between raspy breaths, he said, "You were a virgin."

She turned her head on the mattress and let her eyes slide dreamily over his strong profile. "Yes. But you've changed that."

You're still a virgin because you're waiting to give yourself to the man you love... A child should be conceived and born out of love. I couldn't do it any other way.... Logan didn't know why the words they'd said to each other had reentered his mind at this moment. He didn't want to ponder about any of that now. He didn't want to think about anything at all, except having her next to him.

He grimaced. "I'm not exactly proud of myself."

Smiling, she propped up her head on a bent elbow, then slid her hand across his sweaty chest and down to his flat belly. "You want to undo it? Take it all back?"

He scowled at her. "No, damn it! You know I—" he leaned forward and brought his lips next to hers "—I can't take back or change what just happened."

"I wouldn't want you to," she said softly.

Groaning, he caught her wandering hand and kissed the warm palm. "That's the way you feel now. This minute. But you'll soon hate me for this."

"No," she countered sharply.

He didn't argue with her. Time was slipping by and he didn't want to waste it quarreling. Instead, he pulled the cover up over their naked bodies and pillowed her head on his shoulder.

Logan hadn't intended to doze, but the long night mixed with the drowsy pleasure of having Nicole in his arms caught up with him. When he woke, the first pink streaks of dawn could be seen through the window, and from somewhere in the far distance, a rooster crowed.

Beside him, Nicole's soft warm body was curled into his. He ran his hand down the curve of her back and onto the mound of her hip. She stirred, then her eyes flew open as awareness of where she was sank in.

"I went to sleep," she said, somewhat surprised at herself.

"So did I."

"What time is it?"

"A little before daylight."

She sighed as she realized the night was nearly over. She didn't want it to end. For some unknown reason, she was afraid for it to end.

"Darcy will be here soon," she warned him.

His hands found her breasts and a glow flickered deep in his gray eyes as they searched her face. That he wanted her again amazed Nicole and flooded her with desire.

"Not that soon," he whispered thickly.

Later that morning Nicole hummed a little tune as she poured herself a second cup of coffee. Across the kitchen, Darcy lifted the lid on a pot of boiling beans.

"Sounds like you're in a good mood this mornin'."

Heat filled Nicole's cheeks, but thankfully the other woman was too far away to see it. "I guess I am."

Darcy stirred the beans with a wooden spoon. "Would it have anything to do with that dinner you and Logan had last night?"

Was it only last night that the two of them had gone to Lafayette? she thought. So much had happened in so little time.

"We did have a wonderful time," Nicole admitted to the housekeeper. "Isn't it amazing? A few weeks ago I hated the idea of Logan being here at Belle Rouge, but now I—"

She broke off, not really knowing how to finish the sentence, or even if she should. Her newfound feelings for Logan were too fresh and personal to share with anyone yet.

Darcy shot her a pointed look. "But now you what?"

Shrugging, Nicole lifted the last of a buttered biscuit to her lips. After she swallowed a bite, she said, "Well, you have to admit Logan has changed since he's come home."

Darcy dropped the lid back on the beans, then, tapping a finger thoughtfully beneath her chin, she said, "Uh-huh. I agree the man is a little nicer these days. I don't have any arguments about that. And I'm beginnin' to get the feelin' he cares about this old place. Just like this morning—he barely got his coffee and eggs down before he headed out to the fields."

The second time Nicole woke this morning, she'd found herself alone. She'd known he'd already left for the cane fields. Although he hadn't said much about it, she realized he was worried about the root disease he and Leo had discovered, and she desperately wished she could make things better for him. More than anything she wanted him to be happy.

"I think I hear a 'but' in your voice, Darcy."

The housekeeper walked over to the kitchen table and looked worriedly down at Nicole. "I'm not forgettin' how he treated Mr. Lyle. The man wanted his son livin' here, helpin' him run the plantation, but all Logan could do was judge and condemn him for marryin' your mother. And now he's married you! If that ain't hypocritical, I don't know what is!"

A few weeks ago, Nicole had felt the same as the housekeeper. But that was before he'd come home to Belle Rouge to live, and until then she'd carried around the fixed image of him as a spiteful young man out to hurt his father. In her mind, he'd been nothing but a villain. But now she could see that, like her, he'd been a victim of their parents' illicit love affair.

"That's all true, Darcy. But we're suppose to forgive and forget. And you need to remember that Logan was deeply hurt when he lost his mother, and hurt even more when Lyle married the woman he'd been cheating on Clara with."

Darcy sniffed. "Well, I'll admit Mr. Lyle wasn't no

saint. He didn't always live by the Good Book. But I'm pretty sure Logan ain't, either. That's why I'm mighty afraid he's gonna break your little heart.''

Nicole tried not to let Darcy's chilling words get to her. Logan cared about her. Otherwise, he wouldn't have made love to her like he had. Maybe they had signed a paper saying everything would be over in six months. But after last night, Nicole couldn't believe their marriage would end. In the heat of passion he'd called her Nicki. No one had ever called her by the shortened name, and because Logan was not a man to use endearments, she believed the nickname had been his own way of calling her his darling.

''There's nothing for you to worry about, Darcy. Logan and I understand each other. He might have resented me at one time. I did him. But, well, we've gotten past all that. He would never intentionally hurt me.''

''I hope you're right, Nicole, or me and Sally is gonna run his you-know-what all the way back to Shreveport.''

By midafternoon Logan still hadn't returned to the house. Which wasn't unusual. Many days he stayed out with the farmhands until quitting time in the evening. But Nicole was desperate to see him. She wanted to touch him, kiss him, reassure herself that their night of passion had really happened.

With a wistful sigh, she glanced up from the ledger sheet she'd been working on. What was their life together going to be like now? she wondered. Several times today, she'd started to move her things into his bedroom, but each time she'd stopped herself. She didn't want to be presumptuous in thinking he wanted her to be a real wife to him. But each time she recalled the desperate urgency of his lovemaking she couldn't imagine him wanting anything else.

No, the more she thought about last night, the more certain she was that the two of them had taken a step toward a loving marriage. He'd not bothered to use birth control, and though it had been the wrong time of the month for her to conceive, there wasn't any way Logan could have known that. Just the fact that he'd taken the risk of having a child with her was enough to make her believe he was ready to risk loving her. And that was enough to fill her heart with hope and joy.

He'd lost his mind. That was the only excuse Logan could think of for his behavior last night. What in hell had he been thinking when he'd carried Nicole to his bed? That's just it, he grimly reminded himself. He hadn't been thinking.

But she's your wife. There's nothing wrong with making love to your wife.

The little inner voice shouting back at him made him groan and pinch the bridge of his nose. Every part of him wanted to believe that was true. At this very moment he wanted to rush home, take her in his arms and tell her he wanted them to be together forever.

But he'd told one woman that before, and all he'd gotten from her was laughter. She couldn't marry Logan, she was already married, she'd told him. She was just using him as a bed partner until her husband returned from an extended overseas job.

The shock of learning Tracie was married had been like a physical blow to his body. She'd lied and deceived him in the worst kind of way. Moreover, it had sickened him to know he'd betrayed a man he hadn't even known. True, Logan had done it unwittingly, but the guilt had been there inside him just the same.

Once he'd learned of Tracie's husband, he'd instantly severed ties with her. And to make sure he was never taken for a sucker again, after that he kept his female company light and casual.

Looking back on it now, he realized it wasn't just his anger at Tracie or his guilt toward her husband that had left such an indelible impression on him. The whole thing had made him feel as if he was following in his father's footsteps. A cheater. A man who'd given in to his lust, never worrying about the consequences of who it might eventually hurt.

Of course, Logan knew Nicole wasn't lying to him. She couldn't shock him with a secret husband. Or even a lover. But he couldn't let last night repeat itself. When he touched her, he did it with everything inside him. When he'd made love to her, he'd felt all of himself pouring into her. For the first time in his life, he couldn't keep lust and love separated. Not with Nicole.

His jaw set, he started the engine of the truck and headed out of the cane field. The workers had all gone home, and he'd been sitting at the edge of the river for so long that the night shadows forced him to turn on his headlights.

Ready or not, he had to return to the house. And the image of Nicole waiting for him with her soft arms and warm smile, was like a knife twisting in his gut.

Nicole was sitting on the front porch when Logan's pickup pulled to a halt in the drive. Sally barked and ran out to greet him. Nicole followed the hound at a slower pace. Even so, she was standing outside the door when he opened it and slid to the ground.

"What are you doing?" he asked.

The blunt question took her aback for a moment, but then she smiled and reached for his arm. "Waiting for you, silly. My stomach is growling and Darcy has made red beans and rice."

He didn't reply, but started toward the house, forcing her to release her hold on his arm. She walked beside him, her heart thudding heavily as she cast glances at his bleak face.

"What's wrong?"

Logan could hardly bear to look at her. The soft turquoise shift she was wearing gently touched her curves and exposed her chest and arms. One side was slit up her thigh and each step she took revealed the smooth skin of her leg.

Yet her physical beauty was only a small part of the agony he felt when he looked at Nicole. It was the tender, welcoming smile on her face, the eagerness of her fingers as they'd wrapped around his arms that cut him deeply. She obviously believed they were supposed to be together now. Man and wife.

"Nothing."

She released a small breath. "Oh. Well, that's good. From the look on your face, I thought something bad might have happened."

As they stepped onto the porch, he glanced at her face. She smiled at him again and the sight tore a hole right through his heart. Was he crazier than he first imagined? he asked himself. This beautiful young woman wanted him. She was his wife. Why wasn't that enough?

"I'll...tell you about it after we eat," he said roughly.

Anxious now, she caught him by the arm. "No. If something is wrong, tell me now. Are you ill? Did you hurt yourself today?"

"No. It's..." He groaned with resignation, then reached for her shoulder. "About you and me."

She stared at him. "You mean last night?"

He nodded grimly.

"Oh."

He drew in a long breath and let it out slowly. "It's not going to happen again, Nicole. If you were thinking it was, then...get it out of your mind."

Chapter Eight

Nicole felt as if Logan had whammed her several times in the chest and she'd totally lost her breath. Even when her mother had died, she hadn't felt such intense physical pain.

"I guess—" she let out a shaky sound that was meant to be a laugh "—I got a little confused. But I'm straight about things now."

"Nicole, I—"

Before he could utter another word, she turned and hurried into the house. Upstairs in her bedroom, she locked the door with trembling hands, then walked over to the dressing table and stared at herself in the mirror.

The pain she'd felt down on the porch was beginning to ease just a little. In its place a blessed numbness was creeping in, blotting out the shock of his words. But her legs were quivering so badly she was forced to sink onto the dressing bench.

Leaning closer to the mirror, she was relieved to see

her eyes were dry, her hair still in its smooth chignon, her pink lipstick without a smear.

She'd never thought of herself as a beautiful woman. But neither was she ugly. Her features were regular, her skin smooth, her teeth even and white. She didn't think a man would be embarrassed to be seen with her. And yet she had to accept there was something about her they couldn't love. Her father, Bryce and now Logan.

"Silly girl," she said to the image in the mirror, "you weren't really thinking Logan loved you? He's a man. All he wanted from you was sex. And now he doesn't even want that."

Numbly, she turned on the bench and gazed around her bedroom. Thank goodness her clothes and toiletries were all still in place. If she'd gone ahead and moved them into his bedroom this afternoon as she'd wanted to, her humiliation would have been far greater.

Her head jerked around as a knock sounded on the door.

"Nicole, are you in there?"

She swallowed twice and was proud when her voice came out normal. "Yes. What do you want?"

"Aren't you going to eat supper?"

"No. I…guess I ate too much rich food last night. I don't think my stomach can handle red beans."

He tried the knob and was shocked to find it locked. Nicole never locked a door for any reason. Belle Rouge wasn't a place for locked doors, she'd once told him.

"Are you in there crying?"

The question was like the swipe of an eraser across a blackboard. Suddenly the sad resolution inside her was replaced with fiery anger. How dare he think she cared that much? How dare he be that conceited to have the idea she would cry over him!

Marching over to the door, she flipped the lock and pushed it open. Obviously he wasn't expecting the slab of wood to suddenly swing out at him. He jumped back, his face a picture of surprise.

"Do I look like I'm crying? Do you think you're that great, that wonderful?" Stepping forward, she jabbed a forefinger in the middle of his chest. "Well, you might as well get that out of your mind, buster. I'm not going to fall to pieces just because you don't want to have sex with me!"

Furious, he grabbed her hand, crushing it in the hard grip of his fingers. "Don't try to act like you weren't waiting for me down on the porch."

"I was waiting for you! Why not?" she challenged.

"And don't try to tell me you weren't expecting for us to have supper together and then go to bed."

Her breath was coming hard and fast as her brown eyes scorched a path over his face. "Am I supposed to be ashamed of that?" she asked, then went on before he could answer. "I'm not going to lie to you, Logan. I was looking forward to being with you. In and out of bed. But now you—you've ruined everything!"

"No, last night was when I ruined everything," he corrected.

It was all Nicole could do to keep from hurling herself at him, beating his chest, his face, anything to inflict him with the same humiliating pain he was giving her. But she wasn't a heathen. She was a Southern-bred lady. She couldn't allow him to make her forget that.

"Why?" she asked, the upward tilt of her chin daring him to answer.

"Why?" He spluttered with disbelief. "Are you crazy, Nicole? We're getting a divorce in less than six months!"

"What has that got to do with this? With last night? When you took me to bed you weren't thinking about a divorce!"

A dull red crept across his face. He dropped her hand as though it contaminated him. "And I should add neither were you!"

"I'm not that calculated or cold-blooded. Why should I pretend to be?" she demanded.

Cold-blooded? Just looking at Nicole made his body burn with flames of desire.

"All right, Nicole, I'll be the one to admit this is all my fault. I promised to keep my hands off you. I didn't. I'm sorry. Now all we can do is forget it ever happened!"

Disbelief froze her stare. "Did what we share between us mean so little to you that you can toss the whole incident away? Forget it ever happened?"

A million years wouldn't be long enough for Logan to forget how it had felt to make love to Nicole. Her soft body had turned him inside out. She'd made him forget who he was and where he was. But he would never let her know. He couldn't give her that sort of power over him. His father's life had been controlled by women. Logan sure as hell wasn't going to follow in the old man's footsteps.

"You once assured me you'd never mistake my lust for love," he said accusingly.

The pain that had hit her on the porch was back, but she did her best to hide it. "I might be guilty of being foolish, Logan, but I'm not stupid. I know you don't love me. You never have. You never will."

Nonplussed, he raked a hand through his dark hair. "But—"

Shaking her head, she interrupted. "I thought we had a truce between us. I had the idiotic notion that throughout this six months of marriage we could be close, could give each other joy and companionship instead of this bitterness you can't seem to shed."

His lips twisted. "Sex without commitment. You're not that kind of woman, Nicole."

No, somewhere in the deepest part of her, she knew she'd made love with Logan because her heart had wanted him, loved him. And she'd desperately hoped he might love her, too.

"Maybe you just turned me into one," she said coldly. Turning back into the bedroom, she shut the door in his face.

Hours later, Nicole was about to climb into bed when Logan knocked on the door again. Her heart pounding painfully, she tightened the sash of her robe and moved toward the door.

"I'm going to bed, Logan. Leave me alone."

"Let me in, Nicole."

He wasn't exactly pleading with her. God forbid that Logan would ever plead with anybody, she thought dourly. But he was asking, and if he really wanted in, she could hardly keep him out.

Drawing in a bracing breath, she opened the door to see him holding a tray of food.

"What do you want?"

He stepped past her. "I brought you some supper."

A strange mixture of emotions poured through her as she watched him carefully set the tray on the night-stand beside her bed. He swore he didn't want to be close to her, yet here he was behaving as though he actually cared about her.

"I didn't want any."

"You're always hungry. You never miss a meal."

He sat down in an armchair to the left of the bed and nightstand, making it obvious he didn't plan on leaving immediately.

She sighed. "There's no need for you to feel guilty because I didn't eat. That was my own choice."

"You don't want me to do anything for you. Is that it?"

Seeing it was only going to prolong his stay if she didn't eat, she took a seat on the side of the bed and inspected the tray. There was a bowl of red beans and rice, a smaller bowl of collard greens, two pieces of cornbread and a slice of apple pie. It was one of her very favorite meals, and she had been looking forward to sharing it with Logan. In spite of their shaky relationship, they always ate the evening meal together. But maybe that had never been out of mutual liking. Maybe both of them were simply gluttons for punishment, she thought sadly.

She picked up her fork and slowly began to eat. After she'd finished nearly everything on her plate, Logan said, "I want to talk to you and I want you to listen. Really listen to what I'm about to tell you."

She cut him a sidelong glance. "Surely you've said it all. I certainly know where the two of us stand. You don't have to be worried that I'll be trying to...seduce you."

She didn't have to try, he thought. Just the sight of her, the sound of her voice, the impersonal touch of her hand seduced him.

"You're taking this whole thing personally, Nicole, and that's—"

She put down her fork and turned to him with wide eyes. "Personally? Good heavens, Logan, how much more personal can you get? I realize I'm young and I was a virgin, so tell me, is there something else out there I don't know about? Is there something more that men and women do together before you call it personal?"

He could see her anger was starting to rise again, and that was the last thing he wanted. For them to endure and make it together for the next six months they had to understand each other.

"I'm not talking about any of that! I'm talking about—" He broke off with a groan, then, leaving the chair, eased down beside her on the edge of the mattress.

When he reached for her hand, she jerked it away. "Don't touch me, Logan. Now or ever!"

He knew he deserved her scorn, but it hurt him just the same. Less than twenty-four hours ago, she'd begged him to never stop touching her, and the memory still had the power to tie his insides in knots.

"Don't you understand, Nicole, this isn't about you? You're beautiful, intelligent, desirable—all the things any man would want."

"But you don't."

He suddenly felt flat. "That's right. Because I..." He shook his head and closed his eyes. "I'm thirty-four years old, Nicole. I've never been married and I wouldn't be now if it hadn't been for Dad's will. And that choice has nothing to do with you. I told you once before I don't want to get close to you or any woman."

He'd gotten more than close to her last night, she

thought. But that had been only physical to him. He hadn't felt the same emotional connection as she'd felt. His heart hadn't soared on wings each time she'd touched him.

Her eyes were sad as she looked into his. "In other words, you don't want to love or be loved."

He looked away from her, but not before she saw a dark shutter fall over his face.

"That's right. And I'm not going to take advantage of your body when...you deserve more...better than what I can give you. Just think, Nicole, you might be pregnant now!"

Suddenly her heart was breaking for both of them. "There's no need for you to worry about that. It's far too late in my cycle for me to be pregnant."

The relief on his face stabbed her with fresh pain.

"Thank heavens! I'd never forgive myself for doing that to you. My having a son would keep Belle Rouge and the McNally name going, but I hope you know I'd never use you in such a way. Just to produce an heir. A child should be conceived from love and I just can't..."

"You don't want a child to love," she finished painfully. "You don't want to love anyone. Why?"

With his gaze focused on the opposite wall, she watched the corners of his mouth draw downward. "Because it doesn't last."

"That's not true," she said gently. "I know people who've been in love and married for years."

"Maybe I should have said it wouldn't last for me."

"How do you know?"

He looked at her and his expression was filled with so much anguish it tore right through Nicole.

"Nicki, my own mother couldn't stay sober long enough to notice me, much less love me."

"Lyle loved you."

He groaned. "Maybe in his own way. Once Mom died he turned all his attention to you and Simone. That's why—I guess that's why I tried to buy her off. I felt as though I was losing all my family. When that didn't work, and he married your mother and moved you two into the house, it was like he'd made his choice. He didn't give a damn about me or my feelings in the matter." Logan grimaced and shook his head. "Oh, now I know I was wrong about your mother. She wasn't a gold digger. But I couldn't see that. I was too hurt."

"You should never have left," she said softly.

He nodded. "No. I told myself I didn't need any of you. But I got lonely, Nicki, very lonely. Eventually, I met a woman I thought I loved. I decided that, with her, I could make my own family, that the one at Belle Rouge didn't matter anymore."

Nicole wasn't sure she wanted to hear about his love for a woman. But she had to hear it, she realized. Otherwise she would never understand what drove his heart.

"What happened? Did she die?"

The innocent question elicited a groan from deep within him. Of course Nicole would think in those terms. That only death could end true love.

"No, Nicole. It wasn't anything so tragic. We'd been living together for a while and I decided it was time to ask her to marry me. Her response to that was a fit of laughter. She said, 'Honey, I thought this was just fun and games with us. I've got a husband working overseas. But that doesn't mean we can't enjoy ourselves until he gets back in a few months.'''

"You didn't know?"

"Of course I didn't know! I wanted to kill her, and I hated myself for cheating with some man's wife."

"But you didn't know he existed. It wasn't your fault."

"Oh, yes it was," he said sourly. "I should have had my eyes open. Instead, well...after Tracie, I decided love just wasn't for me. It's too risky. Too painful."

For long moments, she studied his hard profile. "Are you comparing me to her, Logan? How could you?"

He turned his head and met her gaze head-on. "No. I know you're not like her in any way. As I said before, you're not the problem. It's in here." He tapped his chest. "It's with me. I'm not ever going to let myself feel that much for anybody again."

Her head swung back and forth. "That's cowardly."

He rose to his feet and walked to the door. "No, that's playing it safe, Nicki. Now finish your pie and try not to hate me."

Nicole placed the paperback on a nearby table and, from the screened-in veranda on the back of the house, gazed out at the pecan grove. The deep shade invited her to take a stroll beneath the tall trees, but she didn't have the energy to leave her seat on the chaise longue.

For the past two weeks she'd been listless, and her condition wasn't an effect of the humid heat. It wasn't even a physical problem. Her heart and her mind were drained. They were both tired of wondering, thinking, aching for things to be different with Logan.

Damn it, she was going to have to get the man out

of her system. It didn't matter that he was her husband. In his eyes that was just a formality on paper. The ring on her finger meant nothing. The vows they had said to each other had just been repeated words. And their night together had only been sex.

Swinging her legs over the side of the chair, she dropped her face in her hands. The morning was already getting hot, but she didn't want to go inside. The walls of the old house felt as if they were closing in on her, making her wonder how she could possibly continue to live here for five more months.

"So here you are. Darcy said she thought you were out here."

Surprised by the sound of Amelia's voice, Nicole lifted her head.

"Amelia! What are you doing here?"

The woman smiled wryly. "Now that's the sort of gracious, glad-to-see-you greeting I was expecting from you."

Nicole rose to her feet and hugged her friend. "Of course I'm glad to see you. I'm just surprised, that's all."

She motioned for Amelia to take a seat in a nearby wicker chair.

"Oh, I've been down to Alexandria," the other woman explained. "I attended a health seminar there last night. So I stayed over and did a little shopping this morning before I left."

Nicole tried to give her a wide smile, but it was wan at best. "I'm glad you decided to detour over here to Belle Rouge on your way home."

Amelia made herself comfortable in the cushioned chair, then cast a pointed look at Nicole. "You look terrible."

Nicole grimaced. "Thanks. That's just what I needed to hear. Especially from a nurse."

Amelia eyed her shrewdly. "I'm only telling you what I see. You're pale, with dark circles under your eyes and I'd wager you've lost at least ten pounds."

Nicole glanced away from her friend's scrutinizing gaze. "Not nearly ten. And it's been hot."

Amelia made a disgusted sound. "Louisiana is hot for nine months of the year. And you always thrive in the heat. So tell me what's wrong," she urged.

Sighing, Nicole looked back at her friend. "Amelia, you should be down on your knees thanking God that you're not married."

Humor twisted Amelia's red lips. "I assure you I did that very thing when Carl finally gave me a divorce."

"Well, maybe you should do it again, because I don't think you realize how lucky you are," she said, her voice dripping with acid.

Amelia leaned forward in her chair. "What's the matter? Is Logan trying to back out of the deal?"

If only that were the problem, Nicole thought miserably. "No. We've already signed the papers. Legally, everything has been taken care of. All we have to do now is…wait for things to be…over."

Amelia's eyes narrowed as she picked up the quaver in Nicole's last word. "Oh, Nicole, don't tell me you've fallen for the man!"

With a weary sigh, Nicole closed her eyes. What would be the point in trying to lie to Amelia? she asked herself. The woman wasn't stupid or blind.

Groaning with self-disgust, Nicole looked at her friend. "I know it's crazy. And I know I'm a fool. But I can't help it, Amelia. Something happened to me after we were married. I don't know exactly how to explain it, but he began to change a little and I did, too. And suddenly I realized I hadn't really known Logan all these years. Not like I thought I did.''

She sighed heavily and her gaze dropped to her linked hands. She didn't understand why she continued to wear the wedding band he'd given her. It didn't signify commitment or love. All it represented was a barter—her share of Belle Rouge for money. The whole idea had become sickening to her. ''Not like I do now,'' she added sadly.

Amelia's lips compressed to a thin line of disgust. ''So the man couldn't keep his hands off you.''

Nicole groaned. ''It's not that!''

Amelia threw up her hands. ''Honey, I tried to warn you. I didn't miss the way he kissed you after the judge pronounced you man and wife. He's a hundred percent male and you're a beautiful woman. So now he wants you to warm his bed until it's time to throw you out.''

Nicole shook her head. ''No. We're not making love anymore. Logan doesn't think it's right.''

The other woman's brows shot upward. ''Do tell.''

Dropping her head again, Nicole groaned and pinched the bridge of her nose. ''Oh, Amelia, I don't know why I do, but I love the man. And he...he doesn't want to love anybody!''

''Why?''

''I'm not sure. But I don't think he really knows what love is. You remember I told you his mother, Clara, was an alcoholic?''

Amelia nodded and Nicole continued, ''Well, I don't think he ever got much attention or devotion from her. And Lyle was always so caught up with Simone that Logan never got much notice from him, either. Then a woman in Shreveport betrayed him pretty badly and after that...well, I guess he decided no one gave a damn about him and he wasn't going to give a damn about anyone. Ever."

"If that's the way he feels, then you need to wake up and smell the roses, honey. He doesn't want to be serious."

"I know that," Nicole said glumly.

"Good. Then quit taking it so personally. There are millions of men in this world just like him. They don't need or want anyone but themselves."

Nicole slowly rose to her feet and walked over to the screen surrounding the long porch. A few feet away, beneath the deep shade of a magnolia, a jay and a mockingbird were squabbling over a birdbath. As she mindlessly watched the birds, she said, "I know you're right, Amelia, but that doesn't make it any easier to accept."

Amelia studied her for long moments before she said, "The only certain thing I can tell you, Nicole, is that you can't make someone love you. They either do or they don't."

And Logan didn't, Nicole thought with final resolution. "You're right about that," she said quietly, then turned an anguished gaze on her friend. "So what am I going to do, Amelia? I have to stay here until our bargain becomes legal. That's five more months! I can't stay in this house, moping about for that long. And when Logan comes home in the evenings it's...torture."

Amelia shook her head. "Why don't you go ahead and get a job? It's what you've been planning ever since college. What's stopping you?"

"I'm going to have to move in a matter of months

and I don't know where. No employer wants to hire someone who isn't firmly settled."

Amelia frowned, then her face lit up as an idea struck her. "What's wrong with Natchitoches? I've always wanted you to live closer. The town has plenty to offer. I'm sure if you scoured the place, you'd find someone needing an accountant."

Nicole walked back over to the lounge and sank onto its edge so that she was facing Amelia. "Natchitoches is where I'd always planned on working. But now I think it might be better if I got farther away, if you know what I mean."

Amelia leaned forward in her chair. "Why? It's bad enough to let the man run you out of your own home. Why let him dictate where you live?"

Nicole pondered her friend's questions and came up with the conclusion that Amelia was right once again. "You know, I could go see Thorndyke. He and his associates have handled Belle Rouge's estate for years. And he's always offering to help me. He might be able to pull some strings in the way of a job."

An encouraging smile spread over Amelia's face. "Now you're talking more like the Nicole I know. Why don't you go see him this afternoon? Keeping yourself busy and out of this house is just what you need."

Going to work was what she needed, Nicole had to agree. But surprisingly, it wasn't what she really wanted. Once upon a time becoming an accountant, being out in the workforce and being an independent woman, had been her entire goal. Now the thing that would really make her happy was Logan's love. His children. Making a home and family with him. Forever.

Futile, foolish wishes, she thought as she tried to

push the ache out of her heart. If she was ever lucky enough to have love and a family, it wouldn't be with Logan. She had to face that fact and get on with her life.

Rising to her feet, she said to Amelia, "Come on, let's go inside. Darcy will have some iced tea made, and while we have a glass, I'll call Thorndyke's office and see if he can spare me a few minutes this afternoon."

"I'm right behind you, honey."

"I'm so glad you came to see me, Mrs. McNally. I always like to help my clients if I can."

As Nicole faced Thorndyke across his desk, she unconsciously smoothed the hem of her skirt farther down her crossed thighs, unable to stop Logan's words from drifting through her thoughts. *The man was probably wondering if you were wearing panties and just what it would take to get into them.*

She'd wanted to kill him over the remark. Instead they'd ended up in each other's arms. Now she doubted anything would provoke Logan into getting that close to her again.

"Well, thank you for seeing me at such short notice, Mr. Thorndyke."

Smiling, he folded his hands together atop the ink blotter on his desk. "I hope you haven't found a legal problem with the agreement you and Mr. McNally signed a few weeks ago. Mr. Denton told me he explained to both of you that it would be binding."

Just to think about the agreement left her cold. "My visit doesn't concern the contract between me and my husband. Actually, I've decided to put my accounting degree to use and I hoped you might have some idea where I might look for a job."

The man looked totally surprised and Nicole felt a little more than embarrassed. "I'm sorry," she said after a moment, "I realize you're not an employment service. But you've always invited me to come to you if I needed help, and you are connected to many business people in this town."

He waved his hand in the air, then leaned back in his chair. "There's no need for you to apologize, Mrs. McNally. Your stepfather was not only a lifelong client, he was also a dear friend. It pleases me to help his family in any way. I'm just very surprised that you want to go to work. Isn't Logan seeing to your financial needs?"

Those were the only needs he was seeing to. She drew in a long breath and let it out. "Of course. This is just something I need to do for myself."

"Well, let me think for a moment. You've been keeping the books for Belle Rouge for some time now, haven't you?"

Nicole nodded and he tapped a finger thoughtfully against his chin. "Actually, one of our own accountants is going to be leaving any day now. She's expecting a baby and her vacancy will eventually have to be filled."

From behind his glasses, his gaze roamed from the tip of her tawny head to the toe of her beige high heel. Nicole desperately wanted to tell him her body had nothing to do with the way her brain worked. But she kept the remark to herself. She wanted the job. And she'd come to the conclusion that all men were snakes. The best way to deal with them without being bitten was to avoid making them feel threatened.

"Well, I'm sure you understand every firm or company has its own system. But I have a feeling you'd catch on quickly. Could you start next week?"

She was shocked. "Just like that, you're going to hire me?"

An indulgent smile on his face, Thorndyke moved around the desk and reached for her elbow. "Come along, Mrs. McNally. It will be my pleasure to introduce you to some of the staff."

Chapter Nine

From a window in the study, Logan watched Nicole park her car in the drive, then climb the steps at the front of the house. A cocoa-colored dress skimmed her slim figure and high heels made her long legs appear even longer. Judging from her appearance, she'd obviously been to more than the grocery store, he thought dourly.

When he'd come in from the fields a little more than an hour ago, she'd been gone. He'd questioned Darcy about where his wife had been going when she'd left the plantation, but the housekeeper had hemmed and hawed about giving him an answer. The older woman still didn't like him or trust him. At times he considered firing her, but in the end he always tossed the notion aside. She was a fixture here. And for some odd reason it was important to him to win the old woman's respect.

He waited five minutes, thinking Nicole might come to the study to search for him. But he should realize those days were over. She never came around him anymore, unless it was absolutely necessary. And he didn't try to encroach on her privacy. But he missed her company terribly.

For some reason she'd been on his mind even more than usual this evening, making it impossible for him to get any sort of work accomplished. He'd finally told Leo he was quitting for the day. But he'd come home to an empty house—empty of Nicole, anyway—and it scared him to realize how much he hated the place without her in it.

"How much longer till supper, Darcy? I'm starving." Nicole glanced over the housekeeper's shoulder at the skillet of frying okra.

"Oh, maybe twenty minutes. I'll hurry it. I don't want you gettin' unhungry before I can get it on the table. You've been eatin' like a bird here lately."

Nicole tried to smile. "Well, I have a feeling I'm going to be eating more in the days to come."

The woman twisted her head around and gave Nicole a skeptical glance. "And why is that, pray tell? I've been beggin' you to eat. Now you're suddenly hungry."

Nicole crossed to the refrigerator and poured herself a glass of water. After swallowing half of it, she said, "I've got some news."

Planting her hands on her hips, the housekeeper turned away from the stove and looked at Nicole. "Well, I hope it's somethin' that's gonna make you smile. Has Mr. Logan decided to forget this place and head on back to Shreveport?"

"I'm sure you wish I would, Darcy. But there's not a chance of that happening."

At the sound of Logan's voice, both women turned to see him entering the kitchen.

The housekeeper didn't appear to be the least bit disconcerted at having been caught speaking her mind. However, Nicole couldn't remain as cool. At least not on the inside. Not with Logan eyeing her up and down as though she were a specimen under a microscope.

"What's the news, Nicole?"

She hated herself for suddenly being nervous. Even though Logan was her husband legally, he had nothing to do with her life. Or the choices she made for herself. He'd forfeited all rights when he'd told her he wanted nothing to do with her.

She moistened her lips and squared her shoulders. "I've got an accounting job. I start next week."

Darcy squealed and clapped her hands together in glee. Logan's response was quite the opposite. He stared at her blankly, as though he couldn't digest what she'd just told him. Then he stalked over to where she stood.

"Where? Who hired you?"

"Thorndyke and Associates."

Without saying another word, he took her by the arm and led her out of the kitchen.

Nicole waited until they were out of Darcy's earshot before she began to struggle. Jerking her arm loose from his grasp, she whirled on him.

"What are you doing?" she seethed.

"I think I'm the one who should be asking that," he countered. Then, wrapping his steely fingers around her elbow, he said through clenched teeth, "Come on. Let's go to the study. I don't want Darcy hearing this."

"Whatever *this* is, I don't want to hear it, either," Nicole replied tartly as they headed down a short hall-way and into the cool, dim study.

Once inside the room, he released his hold on her,

and it pained him to see how quickly she put a good distance between them.

But that's what you wanted, Logan, an inner voice mocked. *You don't want to be close to Nicole.*

Aloud, he said, "You might not want to hear anything, but I damned sure do. What do you think you're doing, hiring on at Thorndyke's?"

She made a hands-up gesture. "I'm getting on with my life. What do you think I'm doing?"

His lips compressed to a flat line as his gray eyes traveled the luscious length of her. A red-gold wave of hair dipped over one brown eye, while the remainder was swept off her slender neck in a sleek French twist. Her knit dress was cinched in at the waist with a belt of the same color, emphasizing the curves above and below it. The neckline was veed, and nestled in the faint hollow between her breasts was a tiny cross made of seed pearls. There were also drops of pearls hanging from her earlobes, and they danced against her neck as she walked toward him.

Her natural beauty had always bowled Logan over, but this evening she appeared especially beautiful. And it galled the hell out of him that she'd taken pains to look this way for a group of half-cocked lawyers rather than him.

"Aren't you going to answer?" she asked, a vexed expression on her face. "I thought you brought me here to the study to tell me something."

He had. But at this moment all he could think about was taking her into his arms. "I think...you're trying to get back at me."

Her coral-pink lips formed a perfect O. "Get back at you? Are you out of your mind, Logan?"

He was beginning to wonder. Ever since he'd made

love to Nicole everything had changed. All that had once been important to him could barely hold his interest. For years he'd been so certain of how he wanted his life to be. And ultimately, his end goal had been to get his beloved home back. Now he had achieved that. Belle Rouge would be totally his. But at what price? he asked himself. Was losing Nicole worth it?

Damn it all, he'd never had her, he silently admitted.

He let out a heavy breath. "Look, Nicole, I realize we haven't talked much in the past two or three weeks and I know after that night... Well, I understand that you resent me for taking your virginity."

Shaking her head with disbelief, she moved closer. "You don't understand anything about me, Logan. I don't resent you for taking my virginity. That was my gift to give to you. What insulted me was that it meant so little to you." She drew in a sharp breath, then bit down on her lip as the memory of that night threatened to swamp her with emotion. "But that's in the past. I know where you stand. My going to work has nothing to do with trying to spite you. For any reason."

He didn't look one bit convinced. "That night we went to Lafayette you told me you were going to wait about going to work. Until you decided where you were going to live."

The back of her eyes began to sting, forcing her to turn away from him and try to compose herself. "Yes. I did say that. But...well, things are different now."

It shouldn't make any difference to Logan that she'd gone out and found a job. In fact, he should be relieved she was taking steps to separate herself from him even more. But he hated it. Hated the whole idea with a burning passion.

"You mean you don't want to be around me any more than you have to."

She swallowed at the pain building in her throat. "I have to get on with my life, Logan. My taking a job doesn't involve you. And why should it? Like you said, we'll be divorced in a few months."

"And that's what you want?"

The huskily spoken question stunned her. Whirling around, she stared at him with wide brown eyes. "Of course! It's what *you* want. It's what we both agreed to. You don't want a real wife, remember?"

Suddenly it was all too much for Logan. For the past three weeks he'd wanted her, missed her and hated himself for being too afraid to love her.

Before he could stop himself, he took her by the shoulders and tugged her into his arms. "What do you know about it?" he muttered as he planted kisses all over her face. "You don't know how I feel, what it's like for me to see you, smell you, touch you and not make love to you! And now to think of you at Thorndyke's and that lecherous Denton putting his soft hands on you—"

She strained to push herself away from his chest. "No man is going to put his hands on me! Even you!" she said through clenched teeth.

A savage snarl twisted his lips. "Don't lie. You want me. Just as much as I want you."

Nicole had been planning to stomp on his foot, scratch him, anything to make him loosen the grip he had on her. But something in the strange mixture of his words stopped her. Just like her, he couldn't keep himself from wanting her. He'd been going through the same agony that she had, and her heart ached for him just as much as her body did.

"Oh, Logan," she groaned. "I can't pretend. You know I want you."

Like the flip of a switch, his expression softened. His fingertips roamed her cheekbones, forehead, chin, and finally outlined the lush curve of her lips. All the while his eyes worshipped her face. "Precious," he murmured. "So precious."

She closed her eyes, then melted against him as his lips took possession of hers. He kissed her like a man who'd been starved for too long. His eagerness robbed her breath until she had to grip his shoulders to keep from sliding to the floor.

Bending, Logan slid his arms beneath her thighs and lifted her into his arms. As he transported her across the room to a long, leather couch, she recalled the last time he'd carried her like this. She'd made love. He'd had sex. Yet even knowing the chasm between them, she still didn't have the strength to resist him.

On the couch, she wound her arms around his neck and urged his body down over hers. His hands found her breasts, and through the fabric of her dress, he kneaded their fullness. She moaned against his lips and shifted so that their hips were aligned. In spite of his jeans, she could feel his manhood, rock hard and begging to be inside her.

She arched against him, silently inviting his love. He raised his head and looked at her with glazed eyes. "Any minute now Darcy is going to be calling us to supper."

Darcy! The housekeeper was only a few steps down the hallway in the kitchen. Nicole had forgotten all about the woman. Even worse, she'd forgotten the awful, humiliating pain Logan had put her through three weeks ago. She couldn't go through that again. No matter how much she wanted him.

"You're right," she said with quiet resignation. "I'd forgotten about supper and a lot of other things."

He forced himself to ease away from her. She sat up and began to deal with a few tendrils of hair that had fallen onto her neck. A distant expression was slowly masking her face, and he knew she was pulling away from him both mentally and physically.

"What does that mean?"

"It means I..." She turned her head and met his probing gaze. "I almost forgot that none of this means anything to you."

Groaning with frustration, he reached for her. "Nicole, don't try—"

She pulled away from him and quickly left the couch. With her back to him, she blinked her eyes and fought to calm the quaking inside her. "Please, Logan, don't say anything. It hurts me to hear it."

He rose to his feet and went to her. Placing his hands on the back of her shoulders, he said, "I don't want you going to work at Thorndyke's. I'm asking you not to take the job."

Gasping with shock, she spun around to face him. "Not take the job?" she slowly repeated, weighing each word as though she wasn't quite certain he'd said them at all. "How could you ask such a thing of me? How could you, Logan?"

His fingers dipped into the flesh of her shoulders. "Because I...I know how Thorndyke is. He's had mistresses for years. And Denton would like nothing better than to get you in his bed. Heaven only knows what the rest of his troupe are like."

Her eyes began to blaze. "Are you trying to tell me you're jealous?"

"Hell yes! What does it sound like?"

With a snort of contempt, she turned away from him and started toward the door. "Well, that just isn't enough, Logan!"

He lunged after her, but barely missed catching her arm. "What is that supposed to mean?" he demanded.

Pausing, she twisted her head around and glared at him over her shoulder. "It means your being jealous just isn't a good enough reason to keep me home."

Furious, he caught her by the forearm. "It's obvious you're deliberately trying to hurt me. And I'm telling you, Nicole, if you go through with this plan, I'll—"

"You'll what?" she dared. "Divorce me? You're going to do that anyway. Take part of Belle Rouge away from me? Well, you've already done that, too. So what's left for you to hurt me with?"

"You are my wife," he stated flatly. "If nothing else, you should want to respect your husband's wishes."

She tried her best to give him a sarcastic smile, but it was full of sad resignation. "And I would love to respect your wishes. If you really were my husband."

This time when she jerked away from him and walked out the door, Logan didn't go after her. If he did, it would be the end of him.

"Maybe the man really loves you, Nicole. Maybe I've been looking at this whole thing from the wrong angle."

Nicole turned away from the rack of dresses to stare at Amelia. All afternoon the two women had been clothes shopping for Nicole's new job, which would be starting in three more days. At first the other woman had been kind enough to stay off the subject of Logan, but ten minutes ago, she'd let loose in spite of Nicole's objections.

"I can't believe you just said that."

Shrugging one shoulder, Amelia tested the fold of a silk skirt between her thumb and forefinger. "This is nice, Nicole, and the moss color would look great with your hair."

Nicole glanced around the small boutique. Thankfully, there were only two other customers besides themselves, and they were on the opposite side of the room and out of earshot. "Amelia, you're driving me crazy. I tell you I don't want to talk about Logan, then you do anyway. Now you drop a teaser like that, then try to change the subject! Why did you say that about Logan? I thought you didn't like the man. I thought you considered him a black sheep. A cad."

The other woman shrugged again. "Well, I suppose I do have to admit I thought of him in those terms. But now I'm beginning to think I don't know the man at all. I mean, I've only been around him a few times and I've mainly based my opinion on what you've told me about him."

"Do you think I'm lying?" she asked incredulously.

"Of course not! I just happen to think you don't know him, either. I mean, not really, deep down."

Nicole turned back to the dresses and sent a hanger screeching across the rack. "You're wrong about that, Amelia. I do know Logan."

"Look, honey, I know I'm the one who suggested you go to work," she argued in a low tone. "But I'm beginning to think he might really care about you. And if the man asked you to stay home, why go against his wishes and rile him? It will only be for a few more months.''

Nicole couldn't believe her ears. She'd never heard her friend talk this way. In spite of her divorce, Amelia liked men and dated from time to time. She'd even said she would like to marry again someday if the right man came along. But Amelia wasn't one to bow down to the opposite sex for any reason. She believed a woman should have pride and independence.

"He's trying to run my life, Amelia. I can't let him do that! He has no right!''

She sighed. "I understand all that. But he's your husband and…when he asked you not to go to work at Thorndyke's I think he was actually trying to say something else to you.''

"Like what?'' she asked mockingly.

"Like, I love you, Nicole. I need for you to stay home with me.''

"No!'' she said forcefully. Then, dropping her head, she whispered hoarsely, "Logan will never love me. Now let's get out of here. I've done enough shopping for one day.''

"Aren't you going to wait and eat supper with Nicole? She'll be home from work in thirty minutes.''

From his seat at the small kitchen table, Logan scowled at the housekeeper. "No. I've got better things to do than wait around for her.''

Darcy tossed a pile of potato peelings into a garbage pail. "Like what?''

"Don't ask me what. There's too many things to mention.''

"Humph. I guess you like eatin' by yourself. Guess you just like bein' by yourself in general, don't you?''

Leaning back in his chair, he gave Darcy a pointed stare. "You sure are mouthy tonight. Are you trying to make me fire you?"

She sniffed. "Wouldn't make me never no mind if you did." Walking over to the sink, the older woman plunged her hands into the soapy dishwater. "This old house isn't a happy place anymore."

He grabbed up his fork and stabbed it into the pork chop on his plate. "I can't help it because Simone died."

"You think that's the reason Belle Rouge is like a tomb?"

He shot her another moody glance. "I wouldn't be here if the woman was still living. And I'm more than certain you'd like that."

Turning away from the sink to face him, Darcy planted a wet hand on her hip. "When you first came back, Mr. Logan, my heart was willin' to give you another chance. I know things weren't always easy for you around here. You felt like you were pushed out of your own home. And I hated that. I really did. And now that you're here again, you've been workin' real hard. I'll sure admit that much, too."

His expression softened. "So where have I gone wrong in your eyes, Darcy? Obviously I have."

She walked over to the table and sank into the chair that Nicole normally occupied. "It's the way you treat Nicole. It pains me to see you hurtin' her."

Turning his attention to his plate, he said, "If I'm hurting her, I'm not doing it intentionally."

"Maybe. Maybe not. But you'd be a blind man not to see how much she loves you. Don't you care about that?"

Logan felt as if Darcy had flung flaming arrows

straight into his chest. "You're mistaken, Darcy. Nicole doesn't love me."

"She's your wife."

He grunted beneath his breath. "The two of us got married to straighten out the holdings of this estate. Nothing more."

"Maybe it was nothin' more to you. But Nicole took it serious."

He jammed a piece of chop in his mouth and forced himself to chew and swallow. "Yeah, she took it serious, all right. That's why she went to work at Thorndyke's. That's why she's not sitting here eating supper with her husband, because she's so serious about her marriage." Muttering an oath under his breath, he shook his head. "Quit trying to get me confused, Darcy. Hell's bells, we're getting a divorce in a few months, anyway. It's already written on paper. Settled."

Darcy snorted and waved her hand. "Nicole doesn't want that job. She doesn't want a divorce. She's just waitin' on you to come to your senses."

His dark brows shot up. "And do what?"

"Tell her you love her."

Forgetting the half-eaten food on his plate, Logan rose to his feet. "You're a meddling old woman, Darcy. I don't know why Dad allowed you to stay around here all these years. I think when Nicole leaves, you can just make plans to leave with her."

To his irritation, the woman chuckled. "That would fix you right up, wouldn't it, Mr. Logan? This big old house with only you in it. Wouldn't be a female or anyone else around for miles to aggravate you."

"Damn right."

Without saying another word, Darcy pushed herself

to her feet and sauntered back over to the waiting dish-water.

Logan opened his mouth, clamped it shut, then left the room.

When Nicole finally stopped her car out in the drive and climbed the steps, darkness blanketed the plantation. Sally greeted her with a lonely whine. Before entering the house, she bent to pet the hound.

"How's my girl tonight? Lonely?"

The bluetick whined again and pressed herself to Nicole's leg. "I know I've been neglecting you. I'll come out after I eat and we'll go for a walk," she promised the dog.

In the kitchen she found supper waiting in the oven. She filled a plate, then carried it and a cup of coffee over to the table. She didn't wonder if Logan had eaten yet. The days when they'd sat at the little dining table together were long over.

Since she'd been at work, a little more than a week, he'd been even more remote. She doubted he'd said more than ten words to her in as many days. Nicole understood he was angry with her. But she wasn't exactly sure why, other than the fact that she'd refused to obey him.

None of his behavior made sense to her anymore, and she tried her best not to think of it at all. But it was impossible to keep him out of her mind. Even at work, he managed to lever his way into her thoughts.

More than anything, it hurt to be living here with him and yet not really living with him. She missed sharing their thoughts, even the angry ones. She missed seeing him, touching him, making love to him. It was like she was already gone from Belle Rouge without even moving, and she wondered if Amelia might have been right.

Would it really make a difference to Logan if she didn't work at Thorndyke's? If she told him she would give up her job because she loved him?

Nicole pushed away the plaguing problems as best she could and finished the rest of her meal. With the remainder of her coffee in hand, she climbed the stairs and was on the way to her bedroom when she noticed a light on in Logan's room.

As she passed, she paused and glanced inside the open door. To her complete shock, Logan was standing at the foot of the bed, tossing garments into a leather traveling bag.

She stepped across the threshold. "What are you doing?"

He glanced up from his task, then promptly turned his attention back to his packing. "I'm leaving in the morning."

Something in the middle of her chest went as cold as ice. "Leaving? For where?"

"Shreveport."

She moved farther into the room. "Why?"

"I have…some business to do there."

"About the plantation?"

He heaved out a heavy breath. "Yes."

"Why don't you send Leo?"

With a tight grimace, he shoved a pair of jeans into the bag. "Leo's already made one trip. I want to handle it this time myself."

The icy feeling in her chest was turning into raw pain. "You're leaving because of me, aren't you? You're trying to spite me for going to work at Thorndyke's."

He let out a deep groan, then turned to look at her. "Damn it, Nicole, I'm sick of us accusing each other of spite and manipulation. It's not getting us anywhere."

Her mind spinning with questions, she unconsciously moved closer. "How long are you going to be gone?"

He looked away from her and back to the bag on the bed. "A few days. I'm not sure."

"What about the stipulations of the will? Aren't we both supposed to reside here at all times?"

"I'm sure there has to be a clause for emergencies. Anyway, Thorndyke isn't going to know about me being gone for a few days. Unless you tell him." He turned hard gray eyes on her. "Have you two gotten that chummy yet?"

She wasn't going to let his accusations rile her. If there was some remote chance his jealousy was born out of love, she didn't want to be angry with him.

"No. I've yet to talk to the man."

He stepped away from her and rammed his hand through his dark, tousled hair. "I shouldn't have said that. What you do at Thorndyke's doesn't concern me. You made that perfectly clear."

"Logan," she began gently, then stopped as he cut her a scathing glance.

"Let's not rehash the issue, Nicole. I realize you were right. I was trying to act like a husband when I'm...actually nothing to you."

Anguish furrowed her forehead. "How can you say that?"

"Because it's the truth."

With a deep sigh, she glanced around for a place to set her coffee cup. She found a spot on the nightstand beside the telephone, then walked back to where he still stood at the end of the bed.

"Logan, you know it isn't the truth. But you need to lie to yourself to feel better, to make your actions seem right and sensible in your own eyes."

His lips twisted. "You don't know what you're talking about."

She closed the distance between them and placed her hand on his arm. He looked at it and then at her face, as though he feared what she might do next.

"I believe I do," she said with as much courage as she could muster. "Deep down you know that I care about you. And you hate that. It makes you feel trapped and frightened and miserable."

His expression turned mocking. "What could you know about feeling that way?"

"A lot." She turned her back to him as everything inside her began to tremble. "You couldn't believe I was a virgin or that I didn't want a man. You ought to have realized it was because I was afraid."

Long seconds passed and then she felt the gentle warmth of his hands on the back of her shoulders. "Afraid? Of men? What?"

She drew in a deep breath. "Being rejected," she said hoarsely. "You see, you're not the only one who's been through it, Logan. While I was in college, I thought I'd found the guy I wanted to live the rest of my life with. He swore he wanted the same thing. Mother was making tentative wedding plans. But Bryce wanted to bypass the marriage vows for a while and go straight to the bedroom. I refused and that's when the truth came out. He didn't love me. He never had. And he certainly wasn't about to get married."

It was difficult for Logan to imagine Nicole being

so vulnerable and naive. She seemed much too wise a young woman to make herself an open target for heart-ache. But when a person allowed himself to love, he automatically put himself on a one-way track to pain.

"But he led you to believe otherwise?"

"He was a perfect little con man," she said bitterly. "He would talk about where we were going to live and how many children we'd have, the things we would do together. He even took me to meet his parents."

During his college days Logan had known a few guys like that himself, though none of them had lied to such extremes to get what they wanted from their girlfriends. It was no wonder Nicole had believed he was sincere.

"The sorry jerk," he muttered. "Did you ask him why he carried the farce to such an extent?"

She nodded. "He said because I was the hottest little thing he'd ever seen in his life and he was determined to get me."

Just the idea of the unknown man hurting Nicole in such a way had Logan clenching his jaw. "Did you love him?"

She turned and tilted her face up to him. "I used to think so. Until you came home."

His brows drew together in a bewildered frown. "I guess I don't see the connection."

A wan smile touched her lips. "I thought I loved Bryce, but I realize…that was only infatuation com-pared to what I feel for you."

His head swung back and forth. "No. Why are you even saying this?"

Her eyes desperately searched his face. "Because I have to be honest with myself and with you. I thought it might make a difference if you understood that I...love you."

Groaning with anguish, Logan stepped around her and stalked over to an open drawer on the dresser. Rifling through a pile of T-shirts, he said through clenched jaws, "It doesn't make a difference. It won't make a difference."

She'd expected the worst from him and she'd gotten it. Somehow that didn't lessen the pain splintering through her heart, and she wondered a little hysterically if this was the way she was going to feel for the rest of her life.

"Why?" she half whispered.

He didn't look at her. "Nicole, can't you see all of this for yourself? The story you just told me should have been enough to teach you about men and women. It's not love that drives you or me or any of us. It's lust. Pure and simple. And once it dies everything else dies with it."

She walked over to him. "You're wrong, Logan. You just don't want to face the fact that you might need or love someone other than yourself."

He turned away from the drawer and clamped a hand on her shoulder. "I warned you about me, Nicki. Why didn't you listen?"

Utter defeat drained through her like a bucket of dirty water. Biting down on her lip, she looked away from him and drew in a painful breath. "You know," she said sadly, "Amelia reminded me that you can't force a person to love you. It either happens or it doesn't. But she failed to mention that you also can't stop yourself from loving someone. Even a person you shouldn't love."

"Did she also mention how quickly it all ends?"

Nicole looked at him, and for one split second, as his grip on her shoulders eased, a vulnerable shadow clouded his gray eyes.

"Logan, if you care anything about me at all, tell me," she pleaded. "I'll quit the job at Thorndyke's. It's not what I want anyway. I want to be a real wife to you. I want to be the mother of your children."

He swallowed and looked away from her. "Believe me, you'll get over the urge. My mother did. Pretty damn quick."

She wanted to scream at him that she wasn't Clara McNally, but she knew when she was beaten. There wasn't any point in prolonging the fight.

Turning, she headed out of the room. At the threshold, she paused and glanced back at him. "The personal business in Shreveport—is it a woman?"

It wasn't, but Logan knew it was best to let her think so. "A man has to satisfy his urges somewhere."

Her face stone smooth, she walked away from his room and down the steep staircase. Out on the porch, she urged Sally to follow her into the darkness of the pecan grove.

Chapter Ten

"To be honest with you, Logan, this is a puzzler. I've run every test I can think of this week and I can't come up with a reason these cane roots have decayed."

"It has to be the drainage," Logan told the science professor. "Back at Belle Rouge, we tried every sort of chemical we could think of and it hasn't helped."

The gray-headed scientist looked up from his microscope. "And you say the problem is spreading?"

"Slowly. But it has spread." Logan glanced around the college laboratory. For the past week, he'd been waiting, hoping his former colleagues might find a solution to the problem of the wilting cane, but it looked as though the trip had produced nothing.

The older man rose to his feet and clapped an encouraging hand on Logan's shoulder. "Don't look so glum, Logan. At least it's only one field."

Logan frowned. "I didn't want to lose any cane, Cecil. This is my first spring back at the plantation. I wanted this year's crop to be successful."

"Success isn't always measured in amounts."

"So you think I ought to plow up the diseased cane?"

Cecil nodded. "The whole field. Turn it up to the sun and let it bake. Come next spring whatever bacteria is causing the problem will be dead."

"I hate doing that," Logan told him.

The older man gave him a knowing smile. "I'm sure you do. But sometimes you have to let go of the bad to save the good."

Logan grimaced. "You've made your point. Thanks, Cecil. I'll let you know how things turn out."

The two men ambled toward the door leading out of the laboratory. As Logan started to leave, Cecil said, "I'll be looking forward to hearing from you, Logan. And I wish you good luck with your new life at Belle Rouge."

Logan shook the other man's hand. "Thank you, Cecil. I need it. I haven't exactly gotten off to an impressive start." Not with the crops or his wife, he thought dismally.

All week long, he'd tried his best to get Nicole out of his mind. He'd visited old friends, co-workers and places around the city he normally enjoyed. But his old life held no interest for him now. All he could think about was Belle Rouge and the woman he'd left waiting there.

If that meant he was in love, then he had to admit it was the most fierce, persistent feeling he'd ever experienced. He'd tried to shake it, forget it, kill it any way he could. But so far the strange feeling in his heart wouldn't budge and he was beginning to wonder if Nicole had been right. Maybe true love didn't die.

After a final exchange of goodbyes with his old

friend, Logan pushed his way through the door and headed down a wide corridor that would eventually lead him out of the building.

When he reached the parking lot, the late afternoon sun blazed down on his head and shoulders as he unlocked his waiting truck. He was hot, tired and miserable. A week here in Shreveport had done nothing for his state of mind or for his sick cane.

He was going to have to go home and destroy the crop. As for Nicole, he didn't know what he was going to do. Or even if he could do anything. His leaving had probably snapped the last tenuous threads between them.

"Logan! Logan McNally! Is that you?"

He turned away from the truck door to see two women approaching him from the opposite side of the parking lot. At first glance, he couldn't identify either of them. But then the blonde hung back, taking refuge in the shade of a cypress, while the dark-headed one continued toward him. She was less than ten feet away when recognition dawned, sending waves of shock rippling through him.

He'd not seen Tracie since he'd packed his things and left her house all those years ago. Later, he'd heard she'd moved to Biloxi, and he'd been relieved. He hadn't wanted to worry about a chance encounter with her or her husband.

"Logan, it is you!" she squealed. Then, rushing up to him, she grabbed his face with both hands and planted a kiss on his cheek.

Catching her by the wrist, he carefully stepped back. "How are you, Tracie?" he asked quietly.

Her smile was broad as she boldly inspected him from head to toe. "I'm fine, darling. Really fine. And

you look—well, too good for words! I can't believe
I've run into you like this. What luck!''

Luck or fate had to be against him, he thought as he
continued to endure her suggestive gaze. She was still
an attractive woman. Dark, petite, smartly dressed. But
there was a hard-edged look to her face that told him
she'd been living a life of overindulgence.

"I didn't think you were living in Shreveport,'' he
said for want of anything better.

With an airy wave of her hand, she said, "I'm not,
sugar. Just here visiting an old friend. She has some
business on campus today so I came along with her.
You still teaching here?''

"No. I've gone home.''

She giggled as though the word implied he'd gone
hayseed. "I thought you'd always lived here?''

With suddenly clarity Logan realized his home had
never been here. And it had certainly never been with
this woman. It was odd how plainly he could see that
now.

"I live down south of Natchitoches,'' he explained.
"I just happen to be here in Shreveport this week on
business.''

He didn't remember her smile being so catlike.

"Oh, well, that's just great,'' she purred, then
glanced briefly over her shoulder at her friend. "I can
tell Jill to go on without me and we can run over to
the casinos or...something.''

Logan couldn't believe she thought he'd be willing
to pick things up right where they'd left off eight years
ago. "Sorry, Tracie. I'm married now.''

She giggled again, then added in a naughty whisper,
"Don't worry, your wife will never know.''

The image of Nicole's gentle, loving face drifted to

his mind and he realized that to compare her sweetness and goodness to this brittle woman would be insulting. He'd been a fool for lumping her with Tracie and Simone, his mother, and all the other women who'd fallen short in his eyes. Since he'd moved home to Belle Rouge, Nicole had done nothing but give to him. He'd simply been too blind and afraid to accept all the things she'd offered.

His face hard, he said, "She might not know. But I would."

The smile disappeared from Tracie's red lips. "My, my. Still the prude, I see."

Suddenly Logan was very glad Tracie had chosen this day, this very minute to walk across this particular part of the campus. For eight years, she'd been frozen in his memory as the woman he'd loved. He'd somehow let himself believe her only fault was being married. Now he could clearly see she was rotten and selfish through and through.

"Where's your poor husband? Still overseas?"

She laughed harshly. "Robert? I divorced him years ago. I've had two husbands since him."

"No doubt." Logan turned away from her and climbed into the pickup. "Well, I must say seeing you has certainly been enlightening, Tracie."

Not quite understanding his meaning, she perked up and gave him another smile. "Really?"

"Yeah. I can see I made a great escape."

She was still glaring at him as he drove out of the parking lot.

"Thank heavens you're home. I was startin' to worry," Darcy exclaimed as she met Nicole at the front door.

"Why? Is something wrong?" She handed the housekeeper a dripping umbrella, then hurriedly shrugged out of the raincoat she'd tossed over her shoulders before leaving the car.

"No. But it's dark and rainy. I was worried about you out on the slick roads."

The two women headed toward the kitchen. As they walked, Nicole explained, "After work, I ran by a department store to buy a baby gift for the lady whose place I took. Will you wrap it for me later?"

"Sure. What did you get?"

"I played it safe and got diapers. From what I've been told you can never have too many of those."

Nicole didn't go on to tell Darcy she would have been home earlier, but once she'd gotten to the children's department, she'd lingered and daydreamed. As she'd touched the frilly little baby dresses and the tiny jeans and T-shirts, she couldn't stop herself from imagining what it might be like to have a child of her own. Hers and Logan's.

Naturally, in the end, the daydreams had only made her even more sad than she'd already been this past week. There was no chance she would remain Logan's wife, much less be a mother to his child.

"I've got shrimp salad ready for supper. That's all I made. With Mr. Logan still bein' gone, I didn't see any use of cookin' a big meal."

"That's fine, Darcy. The salad will be wonderful. But I think I'll go up and change clothes first. Even though I had the umbrella, I managed to get wet." She started out of the kitchen, then paused at the doorway. "You...didn't hear anything from Logan today, did you?"

"No. Not a word all week."

"I guess he's busy," Nicole replied.

Darcy snorted. "Too busy to pick up the phone?"

"He's trying to find out what's wrong with the cane," she said with a sigh, trying to block from her mind the image of him seeing any of the women he'd known there. The thought of Logan touching another woman, much less making love to her, clawed at her insides, making her sick with jealousy.

Darcy sniffed. "If you ask me, he ought to be tryin' to find out what's wrong with himself first."

Nicole didn't bother to reply. She wasn't in any mood to argue with the housekeeper about Logan. She'd had an especially trying day attempting to straighten out an account that had been neglected for the past six months, not to mention the fact that Denton had stopped by her office on two different occasions. The first time had been for no apparent reason; on the second he'd asked her for a date.

Nicole had coolly reminded him she was married, but he'd laughed and said a business merger didn't count as being really married. She'd wanted to slap him for being so impertinent and presumptuous. And right.

Her marriage to Logan wasn't real. But like a fool she couldn't stop wishing it would be. That's why she had to leave Belle Rouge—before Logan destroyed her hopes and dreams, her very heart.

After changing her office dress for a pair of jeans and a T-shirt, she ate supper, then switched on the television for the local news. She watched the broadcast through the weather report, then turned off the set and went upstairs.

Before Logan had left for Shreveport, she'd thought the house quiet, but with him gone the silence seemed like a tangible thing.

Get use to it, Nicole. This is the way it's going to be. No matter where you go.

On the way to her bedroom, she passed Logan's door. It stood open, the room dark. Nicole paused on the threshold for a moment, her mind reliving the night he'd carried her up the stairs and straight to his bed.

Everyone is ruled by lust, Nicole, including you and me. And when the lust dies, so does everything else.

Maybe Logan was right, she thought sadly. But the ache in her heart didn't feel like lust at all.

Wind was driving the heavy rain against the pickup's windshield, making it impossible to see more than a few feet ahead. Lightning sizzled above the treetops, momentarily illuminating the black asphalt winding ahead of Logan. If he'd had any sense, he would have stopped for a room an hour ago. But the idea of going one more day, even one more hour without seeing Nicole had kept him glued to the wheel.

His lips twisted with irony. A week ago, he'd left for Shreveport with the idea of getting Nicole out of his mind. But strangely, being away from her had worked just the opposite. He'd glimpsed what his life would be without her, and now he could only pray he'd not waited too long to do something about it.

When Logan finally parked in front of the old house, he left his bags in the truck and dashed through the soaking rain. Even though it wasn't yet ten o'clock, the house was dark and quiet. As he walked through the parlor and headed toward the staircase, the chilling notion that Nicole might have packed up and left raced through his mind. But then he remembered her car had been sitting in the driveway.

She could be out with a man. It would serve him

right, he thought grimly, as he climbed the stairs. He'd rejected her time and again. What the hell did he expect? He couldn't expect anything from her. He could only hope.

When he reached her bedroom, his heart sank to his knees. The light was out, yet the flashes of lightning allowed him to see that her bed was empty. She wasn't home.

Sometimes you have to let go of the bad to save the good.

Why hadn't he realized that a long time ago? he wondered. Why had it taken all these weeks of pain for him to see?

Feeling defeated and angry at himself, Logan started to turn away from the open door. Then he saw her. She was sitting in a rocker, her face turned to the storm playing out beyond the wide-paned windows.

Not wanting to frighten her, he called her name as he stepped into the room. She turned her head and her profile was illuminated by more flashes of lightning.

"Logan."

His name came out coolly, as though the sight of him was as dreaded as the black clouds roiling over Belle Rouge.

"I thought you were gone," he said. "Why are you sitting in the dark?"

She'd been in the darkness ever since he'd left. No, she silently corrected, ever since she'd fallen in love with him. It was a place she was getting use to.

Shrugging, she rose to her feet and switched on a small lamp at the head of her bed. "I was watching the storm."

"It's bad. I wasn't sure I was going to make it home without running off the highway."

Even though she told them not to, her eyes feasted on the precious sight of him. He looked ragged and weary—as weary as her crushed heart. A part of her longed to go to him and cradle his haggard face between her palms, but he'd already rejected her so many times she didn't think her heart could stand one more.

"Why were you driving in this kind of weather? Surely there wasn't an emergency for you to get back home. Or have you discovered something urgent about the cane?"

"The cane has to be destroyed." His heart pounded with a strange mixture of fear and joy as he stepped toward her. "But that wasn't my urgency for getting back home. I discovered something about me. And you."

Nonplussed, she stared at him. "Me? I don't know what you could have discovered about me. I'm the same person I was when you left."

"I hope you're right," he said gently.

Something in his face speeded her heartbeat to an anxious thud. "Logan, you're not making any sense. If you hurried home to tell me you've found a woman in Shreveport, there was no need. I'm not going to try to stop you from having an affair. In fact, before you came home this evening I was thinking you and I should have another talk with Thorndyke."

Moving close enough to touch her, he searched her face with his eyes. Nicole's fingers unconsciously pulled the gaping neck of her robe back together.

"And why were you thinking something like that?" he asked. "Has the old man propositioned you?"

There would be time enough later to tell him about Denton. Right now, she wanted to get this heavy weight off her chest. "No. So far he's remained a gentleman. I want us to talk to him about…our living arrangements.''

"What about them?''

His feigned ignorance irritated her to no end. "You know what about them! I'm about to crack. And you're so miserable you went all the way to Shreveport to get away from me." A moan of desperation rose from her throat as she quickly turned her back to him. "I can't keep living here like this, Logan. I don't want you to lose Belle Rouge, but I've got to get out. You won't have to pay me anything for the shares, I'll just live on the money I'm making at Thorndyke's. That's all I need, anyway.''

"I was hoping you still needed me.''

His quietly spoken words stunned her. She turned slowly and looked up at him with bitter disbelief. "Why? So you could kick me down one last time, tell me again how stupid I was for caring about you?''

Before he could answer, she stepped away from him and hurried over to the window. Outside, the storm was still raging, but she had a feeling there was about to be an even wilder storm breaking lose inside her bedroom.

Logan followed her. As he placed his hands on the back of her shoulders, she kept her gaze firmly fixed on the swaying branches of a live oak. Thunder rattled the glass panes, but his touch shook the very core of her.

"I'm the stupid one, Nicole. Throughout the drive home, I kept wondering how I could tell you—how I could explain what a fool I've been.''

Hope tried to flicker in her heart, but she quickly squashed it dead. She was tired of being hurt. So very tired. "About what? Marrying me in the first place?''

He drew in a long breath and let it out. "Yes. For not marrying you for real."

She refused to look at him. Refused to believe he was saying such a thing to her. "You didn't go to Shreveport to figure that out," she said flatly.

His fingers tightened on her shoulders. "No. But I found it out, anyway."

She let out a caustic laugh. "Isn't that rich? Well, it doesn't matter. Our marriage was over before it ever started. It's a done deal. I don't know what happened to you in Shreveport, but whatever it was, you'll get over it. Just like you said, when the lust dies everything else does, too."

He turned her around to face him. "Damn it, Nicole, I want you to forget all that!"

"Why?"

Groaning, he drew her up against him. "Because I love you."

Her eyes filled with pain. "Do you know what I would have given to have heard those words from you even a week ago? Anything! Everything!"

"I know, Nicole," he whispered with regret. "But I didn't know how to say them. I didn't know what they really meant until today."

Her head jerked back and forth in confusion. "Today? How could today be any different than yesterday, or the day we got married? You just don't suddenly start loving someone, Logan!"

"I didn't just start loving you today! I suppose—" He broke off with a groan of frustration. "Hell, Nicole, I think I've always felt something for you. I just didn't know what it was. Even long ago, when you were a teenager, before I left to go away, I felt some odd sort of attraction for you, and for years afterward, I carried you around in my mind."

Unconvinced, she shook her head. "The few times you came back to visit Belle Rouge, you treated me like a leper. You took pains to say nasty, demeaning things to me."

His lips twisted with regret. "That was only because I always felt threatened around you. I didn't want to care about you or have you care about me. I didn't want us to be connected by our parents' marriage or any other way. Because...well, even then I guess I had already decided I didn't want to be loved as a step-brother, a friend or anything. It was safer that way."

Nicole desperately wanted to believe him, but she was afraid to put her hand trustingly out to him, only to have him knock it away.

"Logan, when you left to go to Shreveport—"

"I was determined to get you out of my mind," he finished wryly. "At the time I didn't understand you were already in my heart. I may not have ever under-stood it, if I hadn't run into Tracie."

Nicole's brown eyes widened. "Tracie? You mean the married woman you lived with? You saw her?"

"Quite by chance, I assure you. I was leaving the college campus, walking across the parking lot, when I heard a woman call out my name." He shook his head with amazement. "It had been years since I'd seen her. Actually, since that night I'd discovered she was married."

Nicole tried not to be jealous, but the idea of Logan meeting up with the old flame of his life seared her with the green emotion. "What was she like? I mean...were you still attracted to her?"

Laughing, he gave her shoulders a little shake. "Attracted? Oh, Lord, Nicole. Seeing Tracie again was the best thing that ever happened to me. I felt like someone had unwrapped blinders from my eyes. Oh, she was still pretty, but she was hard and brittle. And as she talked, I kept wondering how I imagined I could have once cared about someone so selfish. I couldn't believe I'd let what she'd done to me influence so many years of my life. She wasn't worth a second thought.'' With a groan of anguish, he pulled Nicole tightly against his chest and threaded his fingers into her hair. ''When I looked at her, all I could think about was your beauty, your gentle warmth, the love you offered so generously. Oh, Nicole, I'm so sorry. Sorry I couldn't accept it before now.''

Her throat was so full of tears, she had to swallow before she could speak. ''I'm sorry, too, Logan.''

He eased her head back far enough to look at her face. ''Nicole, before I left you told me I was wrong about love. You swore there really was such a thing and that if it was true it would last.''

''Yes. I did say that,'' she said, her voice quavering with tears.

''Do you still mean it?'' His hand came up to gently cradle her cheek. ''Do you still love me, Nicole?''

A tear brimmed over and fell onto his thumb. As he wiped yet another one away, she nodded. ''Yes, I love you, Logan. I always will.''

Without a word, he lifted her into his arms and carried her to the bed. After he eased her head back on the pillow, he sat down beside her and took her chin between his thumb and forefinger. ''I've said a lot of terrible things to you before, Nicole, and you never once cried. Now I finally tell you I love you and there're tears on your face. I don't understand.''

She smiled at him. "All of that other stuff wasn't worth shedding a tear over. But now..." Moaning softly, she rose up, curled her arms around his neck and pressed her cheek against his. "You've made me so very happy, Logan."

His arms wrapped tightly around her as he buried his face in the curve of her shoulder. She smelled of sweet lilac, magnolia and roses. She smelled of the South, of Belle Rouge, of home.

"When your mother died and I moved back here, I thought I was doing it for Belle Rouge. I believed I had come back for the plantation. But all the time it was really you." He rested his forehead against hers. "I'm going to have Thorndyke destroy the agreement we signed. We're not getting a divorce."

Her heart brimming with joy, she said in a tearful voice, "No. We're not getting a divorce. And I don't need the money or the shares. All I need is you."

"And the plantation will go equally to our sons and daughters."

Laughing breathlessly, she leaned her head back and looked at him. "You want more than one child? A few days ago you swore you didn't want a family."

He groaned. "A few days ago I was a fool. Now I realize I've wasted so much time. I'm thirty-four years old, Nicole. I've not ever known what it's like to love. To hold my own children and watch them grow. There's so much you can show me. So much we can do together. I want to live every minute of every day to the fullest."

Her lips tilted into a provocative smile. "Then maybe we should quit talking and start living," she suggested.

Logan was only too eager to comply with her

wishes. His lips found the warmth of hers. At the same time his hands eased the silk robe off her shoulders.

The pain and doubts of the past few weeks melted away with their hungry kisses. Even the storm outside was forgotten as clothes landed on the floor and bed-covers became tangled around their eager bodies.

Much later, as Nicole lay cocooned in Logan's arms, he murmured against her ear, "Once again I didn't think about using birth control. You might get pregnant."

"I hope I do."

He eased her face toward his. Her sleepy eyes were full of love for him, and the sight swelled his chest with an emotion too deep to describe.

"What about your job at Thorndyke's?"

"I only took that because I was so miserable. I wanted to be out of the house as much as possible. I thought it might help me get over you."

"Thank heavens it didn't work," he joked, then added soberly, "Nicole, I'm not a selfish man. I realize I was being unreasonable when I demanded you stay home rather than work at Thorndyke's. But I was so damn jealous. I couldn't stand the thought of another man winning your love."

She stroked her index finger along his raspy jaw. "That will never happen," she said assuredly. "And just so you'll know I don't want to keep anything from you, while you were gone to Shreveport, Denton asked me out on a date."

Logan raised himself up on an elbow and looked down at her. "What did you say?"

"I said no. And reminded him I was married."

A chuckle suddenly spilled from him, causing Nicole to arch a wary brow. "What's so funny?"

"Tracie asked me to go out with her."

His statement brought Nicole's head off the pillow. "What did *you* say?"

Grinning, he gently pushed her back. "I said no. And informed her I was a married man. Which didn't really matter to her. She's married, too. To her third or fourth, I'm not sure which. Anyway, I told her it mattered to me. And I think it was at that moment I realized what I felt for you was nothing like the physical attraction I'd once felt for her. It was something far beyond physical and it was much too precious to lose."

"Then I have to be glad you saw the woman," Nicole admitted.

"Speaking of women, I realize I've got a lot of work ahead of me to gain Darcy's forgiveness. The night before I left for Shreveport I told her she could plan on packing her bags and leaving whenever you did. But I wouldn't have let her leave. No more than I would have ever let you walk out of my life. I guess I've always loved the old woman, I just never could show it."

Nicole's lips tilted in an understanding smile. "I think deep down Darcy knows how you feel about her. And I don't expect you'll have to do much apologizing to keep her here with us. All she wants is for me and you to be happy and together."

He eased his head back down beside hers. "Speaking of happy, if working at Thorndyke's makes you that way, then I want you to continue. I realize how long and hard you worked to get your accounting degree. I don't want you to waste it."

With a contented sigh, she snuggled her head onto his shoulder. "I want to be here with you, Logan. And the children I hope we soon have. Later, when they're much older, I'll put my degree to use."

"Are you sure? I don't want you discontented like my mother was."

"Never."

He sighed. "She was a troubled woman. I never wanted to admit that before, but loving you has made me look at life from all sorts of angles."

"I'm sure Lyle never wanted to hurt her," Nicole murmured. "But he needed someone to fill the void made by Clara's neglect. And that someone turned out to be my mother."

Logan's fingers gently combed through the silky hair lying on her white shoulder. "I use to think Dad was a weak man because he allowed a woman to rule his life. But he really wasn't weak at all. In spite of gossip and in spite of his own son's objections, he married the woman he loved."

Tilting his head, Logan placed a kiss on Nicole's forehead. "Funny how all that is so easy to understand now. Because now I know how he felt. Nothing is worthwhile without the right person to share it with. Not even Belle Rouge."

Her lips formed a dreamy smile. "I wonder what your father would think if he could see us now?"

He chuckled softly. "He'd probably say, 'You two took long enough to come to your senses.'"

Her eyes grew wide as wonder filled her face. "Do you think this is what he had in mind when he wrote that crazy will? That we might actually end up falling in love with each other?"

"I didn't think it before. But I'm certain of it now."

"Hmm," Nicole mused aloud. "I wonder how we can ever thank him?"

Raising up on one elbow, Logan grinned down at her. "By keeping this old house filled with love."

Laughing softly, she reached up and tugged his head back down to hers. "My pleasure."

* * * * *

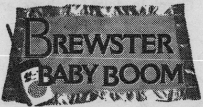

**Start celebrating Silhouette's 20th anniversary
with these 4 special titles by
New York Times bestselling authors**

*Fire and Rain**
by Elizabeth Lowell

King of the Castle
by Heather Graham Pozzessere

*State Secrets**
by Linda Lael Miller

*Paint Me Rainbows**
by Fern Michaels

On sale in December 1999

Plus, a special free book offer inside each title!

Available at your favorite retail outlet
**Also available on audio from Brilliance.*

Silhouette®
™ Where love comes alive**™**